Lust to Kill

After his wife dies, ex-lawman Grant Mayo leaves Texas and travels to Wyoming to make a fresh start. However, he soon finds himself in a land terrorized by vigilantes. A man imbued with an evil lust to kill holds the town of Barclay in a grip of fear. Grant Mayo is the only person brave enough to stand against him.

But he has bitten off more than he anticipated and is drawn into a maelstrom of gunfights, lynchings, murder, abduction, and hot-blooded women. Grant is left with the ultimate test of his life – to pit his wits, single-handed, against the man who has turned the territory into a killing field. It will be a duel to the death.

Lust to Kill

MARK BANNERMAN

A Black Horse Western

ROBERT HALE · LONDON

ISBN 0 7090 7345 3

Robert Hale Limited
Clerkenwell House
Clerkenwell Green
London EC1R 0HT

This one is for
Bill Williams
A Friend in a Million

Typeset by
Derek Doyle & Associates, Liverpool.
Printed and bound in Great Britain by
Antony Rowe Limited, Wiltshire

ONE

'Young man, I know hanging isn't a nice experience,' Doctor Brininstool said, his breath clouding white in the frigid Wyoming air, 'but at least you can take heart in the fact that your dying won't be wasted.'

'Why not?' Grant Mayo croaked faintly, his voice coming from between unmoving lips. His jaw was swollen up like a badly bruised melon. He had found talking difficult as he had struggled to protest his innocence earlier. Now, he was slumped on the snowy ground, his wrists bound behind his back, his ankles secured. He was watching how one of the posse, Stumpy Simmons, so called because of his short legs, was throwing a rope over the branch of an elm tree on the ridge above, testing its strength. Simmons had slipped twice on the icy slope as he'd climbed to the tree, but had pressed on as if his task was the most important duty in the world. Another man loomed over Grant with a Springfield pointed at him. It was ludicrous, threatening to shoot him when he was about to be lynched, although, on reflection, a shot in the head might have been preferable to the choke. It would undoubtedly come if he attempted to get away, but being tied up and

5

severely handicapped by a cracked jaw, his chances were limited.

The rest of the posse was grouped down the slope around a small fire, the bright yellow of their Fishbrand slickers contrasting with the gloom of the day. They were scalding their lips as they drank coffee from tin cups, talking in raucous and profane voices, their laughter jarring the wintry silence of that gaunt land and the depths of Grant's despair.

Further off, the Union Pacific Railroad showed darkly against the snow, curving around the hillside, giving no indication that it had been ruptured at one point.

Forty-year-old Seth Fryer was chairman of the vigilante committee. He was a giant of a man, bulky and clumsy, his considerable girth not disproportionate to the rest of him, and he was made to seem even bigger in his thick, wide-waled corduroy coat and high-crowned hat. His high-bridged nose was like a hawk's beak. His eyes were set wide apart and considerably back in their sockets, sheltering beneath his overhung brow, depriving his face of normal expression. In his youth, he had been taunted for his ugliness, and this had planted black, merciless hatred in his heart.

He paced splay-footed up and down on the slope, keeping apart from the others. His breath froze in the air about him, reflecting how his respiration had quickened. His whole, big-boned body was tingling with excitement for he was about to experience his greatest joy, that of seeing the life fade from a man's eyes. The proximity of death fascinated him. Even as a child, he'd delighted in torturing and killing animals, throwing wretched dogs and goats from a cliff-top, but he had long since moved on to more satisfying victims. Being chairman of the vigilante committee had given him the mantle he relished wearing – that of an executioner, a godlike power over life and death, and all in the name of so-called law. He carried a dragoon pistol, the Civil War model. It fired big, conical shells that could shock a man to death, even if only striking his arm or leg. He grunted with pleasure. Let his men make the most of this last-minute respite before they got down to the real work of the morning.

Doctor Brininstool was a plump, fussy man with heavy burnsides and a moustache. He wore an over-tight coat and scotch-hat, a relic from his days as an army surgeon. His flabby cheeks were reddened by the cold. The previous evening, in the town of Barclay, he had got word that outlaws were planning to derail a train some ten miles along the track and that Seth Fryer was raising a posse in an attempt to forestall the mischief. Brininstool immediately saw his chance. He asked Fryer's permission to join the posse and this was given. He then called out Joe Evans, his apprentice, who looked so much younger that his eighteen years, and they linked with the vigilantes as they rode from town.

During the chaotic hours that followed, one man, Grant, was apprehended. His punishment would come swiftly – just as soon as the coffee was cool enough to drink and the rope had been properly fixed.

'*Why* won't my dying be wasted?' Grant repeated, grimacing at the pain that talking caused to his swollen jaw.

7

'Because Seth Fryer's granted me the right to take possession of your body, to use it for medical research. I'm doing a study into how the brains of outlaws work, what makes them criminals.' Brininstool touched Grant's head, probing the crown with cold fingers. 'Thick spot here,' he observed. 'Rest of it's much thinner. I reckon that indicates very small mentality. You can't help it, mind. The bone and aponeurosis are pressed inward, so the grey matter hasn't had room to expand like it does in normal folk. That's why you turned into a criminal.'

'I'm not a criminal,' Grant managed to gasp. 'Never broken a law in my life. I was once a deputy myself.'

'No matter.' Brininstool hardly seemed to hear the words. He was busy relishing the moment when he could bring his surgeon's saw to bear, removing the top of the skull and studying what was inside. It would be like opening Pandora's box. Could be, after he'd finished his research, he would wire the skull back together, have the corpse preserved and sell it to some fairground proprietor for exhibition. Folks liked that sort of thing. It gave them a moral education and showed them the futility of criminal ways.

'Anyway,' Grant complained, 'it's my jaw that's hurting.'

Brininstool sighed, distracted from his scientific speculation. He leaned forward. 'Try to open your mouth, young man.'

Grant managed to part his lips by about half an inch, and the doctor slipped his finger into his mouth, pressing it against the jawbone. With the other hand he probed his patient's cheek. He found a tender spot,

8

exerted pressure and heard a crunching of bone. Grant howled with pain; it was so loud that the men down the slope stopped talking, glanced up towards him, and then resumed sipping their coffee. Grant had closed his teeth on the doctor's fingers, but his bite lacked power. Brininstool withdrew his hand, shaking it as if to dispel the hurt.

'No need for violence when somebody's trying to help you,' he said. 'Obvious crepitus, no doubt about it. Fracture of the lower mandible. You're lucky there's no haemorrhaging. Jaw needs wiring up and stabilizing.' He coughed, then added, 'But under the circumstances, I guess it won't be worthwhile.'

'Noose is ready!' Simmons called down from where he'd been fixing the rope.

Seth Fryer gave his men a meaningful nod and there was a hissing of flames as they rose from their haunches and discarded their coffee dregs on the fire. Soon the group was scrambling up the slope, one of them leading a nervy bay mare.

High above, a turkey buzzard gaggled its bald head in and out and hung on its wings.

Fryer was regretting the rare gesture of goodwill he'd shown regarding the disposal of the body. His eyes paused momentarily on Grant. He licked his lips, then spat. He approached Doctor Brininstool, looming over him like a grizzly bear.

'I've reconsidered,' he said in his deep voice, 'about letting you take the corpse, I mean. I've decided I best keep it for identification purposes.'

Brininstool's porcine eyes blazed resentment. He was one of the few men who was not overawed by Fryer. 'No, sir! You gave your word. I've never known you break your word before and I won't let you start now!'

Fryer gave his great head a shake. 'We'll see.'

By now events were moving. Grant had been seized by ruthless hands, dragged to his feet, his mumbled protests drowned out by the frenzy of shouting that was spreading through the mob. The prospect of a hanging lifted men's spirits in a mawkish way. 'This'll teach you not to rob trains, not to murder innocent folks!' And: 'Let's get the bastard strung up so's we can go home out o' the cold!'

With feverish haste, the ropes binding Grant's feet were untied, and, his hands still fastened behind his back, he was bundled up the slope, treading in the steaming dung of the bay horse. The animal was prancing and highly agitated, showing the whites of its eyes as if suspecting that it was to be the victim in this execution. Ahead loomed the solitary elm, its branch sticking out like a giant thumb, the noose dangling down.

The spooked mare, voiding its bowels in noisy squirts, was forced to stand beneath the rope, one of the posse struggling to hold its head steady while Grant was hoisted into the saddle. Simmons had to support the condemned man to prevent him from toppling off. The noose was lowered, drawn tight about Grant's neck.

Seth Fryer was in his ecstatic world, savouring his power, enjoying it like sensual exultation, then he raised his voice. 'Let 'im swing, boys!'

The bay mare was released, not needing the whacking of hats against its flanks to send it surging forward from between Grant's legs, and men's voices were raised in a cheer.

Grant dropped like a sack of rocks, his head jerked upward, but simultaneously there was an almighty crack, and he fell to the ground accompanied by the snapped-off branch of the old tree. Cheering voices changed to a stridency of cursing and blaspheming.

Seth Fryer turned on Simmons, his fury striking the smaller man like a blast of flame, making him shrivel back. 'Goddamit, Simmons! I told you to make sure the rope was fixed right! You deserve lynching your damned self!'

'But, Mr Fryer, sir, there was no way I could tell the branch was rotten. I sure tested it . . .'

Grant was slumped on the ground, his eyes glazed, but through his lips came a faint whispering. He was praying and murmuring the name of Josephine, his deceased wife, as if he envisaged meeting her.

'Well,' Fryer growled, 'let's find another tree quick and get the job done properly. Look, yonder.' He pointed to a cottonwood, some fifty yards along the ridge and there was a grunting of agreement.

A man said, 'Catch the horse so we can get on with it!' and another ran towards where the mare stood trembling, its freezing breath coming in white plumes. It tried to bolt and by the time it had been calmed, Grant's lanky body had been lifted and was being carried to the further tree. This time Fryer himself made sure the right branch was found, that it wasn't rotten. He then inspected the rope, testing its strength, before it was tossed over. After executions, he liked to keep the rope as a memento, savouring the feel of the strands as others would the feel of money. Again the horse was led forward, positioned appropriately as Grant was restored to the astride position. He was doubled over, seemingly unconscious, but was drawn up as the noose was lowered over his head for a second time and drawn tight.

This time Seth Fryer did not delay. As the mare was released, Grant dropped and swung for a moment, then a shudder went through his body and his feet began to kick.

Fryer's voice came as a scream. 'Drag on his damned legs, Simmons!'

Simmons sparked into life. 'A pleasure, Mr Fryer!' He struggled to grasp the swinging limbs, grabbing one by the boot which immediately slipped off, dumping his stubby-legged frame in the snow amid guffaws of laughter, though not from the unsmiling Fryer.

Two other men stepped in, catching the still-kicking legs, pitching their weight in a downward pull. Eventually, they stood back.

Eyes half-closed, Seth Fryer was panting like a beast, spittled lips drawn from his teeth in a snarl. His gaze gloated on the now motionless Grant.

'One damned outlaw less!' somebody commented, and there was a surge of acquiescence.

Fryer's gaze remained on the body. He cursed himself for giving his word to the doctor, but even now Brininstool had sent his apprentice eighteen-year-old Joe Evans shinning up the tree to cut the rope. Standing beneath, the doctor caught the body as it dropped, gently lowered it to the ground, and, feeling Fryer looming over him and about to retract his earlier promise, rapidly satisfied himself that life was extinct.

Assured, he straightened up, telling Joe Evans to fetch a blanket. 'We got to wrap him up before he freezes solid and get him on the back of your horse, Joe.'

The apprentice hurried to comply, wide-eyed and feeling downright sick at what he had witnessed. He'd ventured into this employment to save lives, not to destroy them.

Fryer was now desperate to take possession of the body, but Brininstool was determined. 'You gave your word, Fryer. No escaping from that!' and before the chairman of the vigilantes could respond, he and the boy were scrambling away down the slope, carrying the blanket-shrouded body of Grant.

'He sure is dead weight, Doctor Brininstool, sir,' the boy gasped, and then he added, 'Poor devil.'

Somehow, they got their burden to where the horses had been left, got it hoisted across the back of Evans's horse and made secure. Evans himself rode double with the doctor and they led the laden animal. As they headed along the snow-thick trail towards town, the posse overtook them, Fryer giving them a long glare, obviously still regretting his earlier promise concerning the body.

But Brininstool ignored him, setting his mind on the interesting task ahead.

It was mid-afternoon when they eventually reached Barclay, and the swirling snow was borne on a bullying wind, blocking out the light. Within ten minutes, the doctor had unloaded the body, lifted it into his surgery and laid it out upon his cutting-table. He removed his coat, shook it, hung it up and rolled back his sleeves. He had been wearing a gun, a heavy, single-action Peacemaker. He now unstrapped it and placed on the side dresser. He disliked guns, though he had to admit gunshot wounds had kept him in business for a good many years.

The room, lit and tainted by flickering kerosene, was equipped with specimen-jars, surgical knives and all the impedimenta associated with the scientific research that was his monomania.

Joe Evans shuddered as Brininstool pulled away the blanket and gazed at the body.

'I ain't n-never seen a dead man like this before,' the boy stammered, running an anxious hand through his red hair. 'Not lying there, waiting to have his skull sliced open, I mean.'

The doctor had leaned over the body, his expression one of incredulity. He checked Grant's pulse, pressed his stethoscope against his chest, and then his incredulity was gone and replaced with red-faced anger.

'You haven't seen a dead man, not even now,' he growled. 'This fellow's still breathing!' He steadied himself, wiped the back of his hand across his brow, then added, 'But it won't take much to finish him off'

TWO

It was forty-eight hours earlier when Benjamin Hendrix and his six desperadoes had made cold camp in the rocks overlooking the north side of the railroad. Behind them loomed the towering, white summit known as Pilgrim's Pinnacle. They had a clear view of the steel track and of the flat ground adjacent to it. The whole deathful land was deserted. Not a medicine wolf, or even a hawk, showed itself in the cold.

'Plenty of room for the locomotive to run off-track,' Hendrix observed as he slipped from his saddle. He was confident in the plans he'd made. After all, Jesse James had worked the same trick a couple of years ago and Hendrix considered Jesse nothing more than an upstart.

Hendrix was a short man, approaching forty, but his thick body gave the impression of power. His face possessed a strange, passive look, which belied the ruthlessness that he had shown more than once. While undertaking professional work of this nature, his victims were never favoured with a glimpse of his face, for generally it was hidden by a mask of patterned calico, as were those of his men. There could be no portrayal of their features in the Wanted notices that adorned the territory. This was especially important now that he was operating in his own back yard.

All the members of the gang showed Hendrix considerable deference, fearing to arouse his wrath, which was always garnished with piety, and that crossing him could somehow condemn their souls to hell. They were a motley group of hardened outlaws, mostly with Confederate backgrounds, and most of them had participated in plundering banks, robbing stage-coaches, raping women, murdering innocents and stealing horses. This was to be their first attempt at wrecking a train.

They intended to scatter after the loot had been divided, each disappearing to his own retreat as the hue and cry followed its course. When the time was ripe for another job, Hendrix would notify them where to meet up. However, if there was as much cash aboard this train as they anticipated, there would be no further need to risk their necks for a long time.

Now they camped without fire, huddled in their coats, playing poker or arguing as the hours dragged by. But Hendrix was not part of this. He abhorred the gambling and course language of these men. He walked the bleak landscape, inspecting various parts of the track and generally pondering on what lay ahead. But come noon he was well hidden in the rocks as a freight train rumbled through, smoke from its stack staining the icy air. He knew that the next train to appear would be the one they were concerned with. Its security car would be carrying an army payroll. He had paid well for this information and knew that there was no doubt as to its authenticity.

With the freight train gone, he roused his men from their time-passing activities. They unloaded their tools and Hendrix personally led two of them, Dutch and Miller, down to the point where the track went into a down-slope curve. He could have used more men for the work, but considered it unwise to leave a multitude of boot-prints in the snow. He supervized as Dutch and Miller used iron bars to lever the spikes out of the ties on the north-side rail, the clang of metal against metal causing sparks to fly, and seeming awesomely loud in the otherwise funereal silence. Presently they looped the rail with wire, unrolling a fifty-yard length to the side, hiding it by kicking snow over it. When the train approached, they would be able to tug the rail out of line, just an inch or so, and send the engine and coal-car careering to the side.

Once their work was completed, they did all they could to conceal the evidence of their presence, scuffing the snow across, thankful that it was frozen pretty hard and their tracks were not deep. Furthermore, as they returned towards their camp, more snow was falling which was all to their advantage. Back in the rocks with the others, Hendrix looked at his pocket-watch. It was now just after 3 p.m. The train was due at six.

The next hour was spent checking horses, weapons and ammunition, and afterwards Hendrix went over their plan, instructing every man individually, ensuring that the operation would go like clockwork. His men listened to him with heads bowed, almost as if they were on the listening end of a sermon. He was a perfectionist by nature and anybody who did not adopt the same attitude, or was slow to get his message, regretted it.

He had just finished when his second in command, Frank Clayton, called down from the elevated rock from which he had been watching the landscape. 'Boss, there's something coming along the track!'

Hendrix gazed heavenward in frustration, as if reproaching the Lord for not providing him with appropriate support. He hauled himself up alongside Clayton, peering through the curtain of snow. Movement was immediately evident. A handcar was coming along the track, speeding through the murk like a furtive mouse. It was being manually propelled by one man and heading towards Barclay.

'He'll probably spot the wiring,' Clayton gasped, raising his rifle. 'I figure we should shoot him.'

Grant was twenty-three years old and already widowed. He was broad-shouldered and slim-hipped, with an aquiline nose and firm jaw. His skin had been browned by the Texas sun. He was a quiet man most of the time, but energy coiled inside him, hidden until needed. He was employed by the railroad as a section foreman, and was proud of the fine company cap he'd been issued with. It was his job to check the tracks for damage. He was new to this section. He'd worked in his native Texas previously, where winter temperatures were not so extreme. As a youngster, he'd served as a deputy town sheriff before being persuaded by his wife Josephine to quit holding himself up as a target for drunken cowboys. Thereafter, he'd worked in Texas on the railroad, but then, after Josephine died, he'd come to

Wyoming to escape his grief and make a fresh start. Right now he was cursing his luck, being out in such foul weather. He reckoned he thoroughly deserved the increased wages his move had brought. Even so, he was not feeling the cold. Pumping the lever of the handcar raised a heavy sweat.

He was blessed with sharp eyes. Although the car passed over the ruptured rail with hardly a bump, he spotted the way the rail had been loosened, how a wire led off into the snow. His pulse quickened as he guessed what was afoot. Something else troubled him too. If a robbery was intended, as appeared obvious, the outlaws were probably in the close vicinity, maybe even watching him as he worked his cumbersome vehicle. Those rocks on the north side, under Pilgrim's Pinnacle, would be an ideal hiding-place for anybody spying on him. He knew he was a sitting target.

The hairs on the nape of his neck were tingling as he proceeded. His instinct was to pump the car to maximum speed, but he restrained himself. Such action could well bring a hail of lead. He held back on his jangling senses, forcing himself to act as if he hadn't noticed the loosened rail. He neither quickened nor slowed his speed. One thing was certain: he had to carry warning to Barclay, The train must be stopped before it thundered off-track.

From their rocky viewpoint, the outlaws watched uneasily. This was something Hendrix had not foreseen, never having figured the railroad would take such precautions of inspecting the line.

As the handcar came abreast, Clayton lifted his rifle into his shoulder, taking aim at the intruder, but before

19

his finger tightened on the trigger, Hendrix pushed the weapon off target.

'Let him be,' he hissed. 'If he doesn't turn up in Barclay, they'll probably come looking for him. Best to let him go through. Doesn't look as if he's spotted the track anyway.'

Clayton gave a reluctant nod and lowered his rifle. He didn't agree with his boss, but he wasn't going to cross him.

His doubts would have been even greater if he had known that once the handcar had moved out of sight around the hill, its driver had forced it forward at pell-mell speed, using every ounce of strength he could muster as he hurtled through the snowstorm.

He made the ten miles to Barclay at what must have been record speed, his appearance more like a snow-man's than that of a railroad employee. The day's light was fading fast. As he approached the dimly lit station, he saw that the train was at the platform, building up steam in readiness for departure. He hauled his hand-car to a halt, removed his gloves and lit his red lamp. Waving it frantically, he attracted the attention of the driver, glad to recognize him as a man he knew, Hugo Eriksson. Soon, he was panting out his warning, giving details of the line disruption close to Pilgrim's Pinnacle. Hugo Eriksson immediately sent a message to Barclay's self-appointed law-enforcers.

That night, it wasn't the train that left Barclay, but a posse of vigilantes, intent on bringing outlaws to justice. Doctor Brininstool and his assistant Joe Evans accompanied them, as did Grant, having been loaned a horse and coming to provide further information if required, and to protect the interests of the company. Seth Fryer had ensured that they took with them a plentiful supply of rope.

THREE

They rode hard through the bitter night, each man huddled in his coat and muskrat cap, with scarves drawn up to prevent ears and face freezing. The snow soon formed a blanket on humans and horses. Grant found himself at the rear of the riders. As the ride continued, nobody seemed interested in him. The sorrel mare he was riding was not in the best shape and in the severe conditions was soon lagging behind the others. Grant was not overly concerned. While they kept to the trail, he could follow them easily enough.

Seth Fryer was familiar with this country, even in coal-pit darkness and a howling blizzard, and an hour after starting out, he was leading half his men away from the trail and into the rough country of rocks and crevasses. The remainder of his force continued up the trail towards the area between the rail-track and the rocks. They hoped they would be able to shoot down any outlaws who attempted to escape. With luck, they would catch the robbers by surprise, before they had become too suspicious over the non-arrival of the train. Of course there was always the chance that they might have taken flight already and Seth Fryer cursed at this prospect. He reminded himself that the townsfolk of Barclay expected him to bring wrongdoers to justice, a task he was desperate to perform. Oh yes!

They approached Pilgrim's Pinnacle from the north, not being able to see the towering summit in the gloomy night. Fryer had his posse dismount and stationed one man to look after the horses while the rest of the party proceeded on foot, their guns drawn at the ready. They moved in single file, clambering through a snow-clogged gully, Fryer in the lead, the others, including the breathless Doctor Brininstool and his boy Joe Evans, striving to keep up. For fifteen minutes they laboured on until they sensed rather than saw the great slab of Pilgrim's Pinnacle looming over them. It was then, from somewhere ahead, that they heard the nervous snort of a horse and Fryer grunted with satisfaction. His surmising was proving right. Hopefully, in view of the inclement weather, his quarry had holed up, no doubt sickened by the fact that their intended robbery was not materializing. But, in assuming this, Fryer had underestimated his adversaries.

As the posse mounted the slope, the night was split open by the crackling spark of gunfire from both flanks and bullets whanged about men's ears and clipped the bark from trees.

Fryer and his men immediately went to ground, sprawling in the snow, thankful for the screening darkness. They started to retaliate, firing at the spots where the shots had come from, and for a minute there was a spiteful whine of lead. Then the barrage petered out as men took stock of what had happened, and the sudden silence was broken only by the howling wind and the groaning of the posseman, Fairfax, who'd been clipped by a bullet.

Fryer heard the movement of horses up the slope and the dread rose in him that he had been outfoxed, that the outlaws were escaping. The thought goaded him into action. He grunted orders to those nearest him, instructing them to follow him. He then told the others to circle round to the front of Pilgrim's Pinnacle and move mighty quick. Maybe, together with the possemen coming from the south, he could catch his quarry in a pincer trap. The danger might be that the posse would end up shooting each other down, but that was a chance that didn't overly concern him.

Grant had relinquished all hope of keeping up with his fellows, his mare growing slower by each hard-won mile. He reached the point where Fryer had split his force, and decided to follow the group that had swung off-trail. As he proceeded, he heard the racket of shots from ahead and drew up, listening until the gunfire died into the howl of the wind. He waited some ten minutes, shivering in the cold, not wishing to blunder into any crossfire. He wondered if he was now surplus to requirements; his ability to indicate the spot where the rails had been disrupted had not been utilized. But on impulse he decided to carry on, to link once more with the vigilantes and be of any assistance he could. That decision was to cost him dearly.

As rider and horse got nearer to Pilgrim's Pinnacle, gunfire from ahead erupted again, and Grant heard men calling to each other and heard the scurry of movement in the darkness. Then, like a chaotic rush of water, the pound of hoofs sounded so thunderously that he sensed he was about to be run down. As he drew his mare to the side, the darkness seemed to split open before him and shadowy riders swept down the slope, discharging their revolvers in rapid fire over their shoulders. Within a half-minute they had been swallowed up by the night. Behind them, he heard Seth Fryer's voice booming out, urging at his men to give chase.

Grant realized that he was in a dangerous position, might be caught by a random bullet at any second, or could easily be mistaken for an outlaw. He determined to establish his presence to the vigilantes and heeled his mount into motion. It was at that moment that the pounding of hoofs sounded again, rising to seemingly deafening proportions, and a rider and horse burst out of the darkness at a crazy down-slope gallop. Grant was helpless to avoid the impact that followed, having no escape as horse struck horse in a sickening thud. He was briefly aware of being hurled from his saddle, of hitting the ground with bone-jarring impact.

Hendrix was also taken completely by surprise, having chosen to fight a rearguard action. He had been more concerned about pursuit rather than a sudden obstruction to his headlong flight, the belief that he would be able to shake off his enemies uppermost in his mind. Like Grant, he was hurled from his saddle by the collision, his mount slumping to its knees. The beast recovered and bolted off into the gloom. The snow cushioned Hendrix's fall and he staggered up almost immediately, seeing the movement of a shadowy figure before him. Sensing that this man was not from his own gang, he would have shot him down, but his gun had fallen from his grasp in the fall. Grant had scrambled up, was lunging towards him as if to grab him. The two locked arms, struggling – and in that struggle, Hendrix found his calico mask snatched away from his face. For a second his eyes met those of the other man, young, blazing with fury, close enough to distinguish his features despite the gloom. Then Hendrix brought his knee up into his opponent's groin, missing the vital spot but sending him stumbling. Hendrix lunged at him and caught him a crunching blow, finding the point of his jaw, feeling the bone go. Grant dropped, lying still upon the ground as if dead.

Hendrix could hear movement around him, men surging across the slope. They were so close he could distinguish the laboured rasp of their breathing. He expected at any moment to hear the snap of more gunfire, this time directed at him. He was angry with himself for allowing the line foreman to proceed and thwart the robbery, somehow sensing that the man was the very one he had grappled with. Knowing that he was surrounded, Hendrix adopted a desperate ruse. He ripped the bandanna from his neck and dropped down on to his knees. He fastened the bandanna over the face of the unconscious man, knotting it firmly behind his neck. He also changed hats, placing the man's railway cap upon his own head, pulling it down about his ears.

At that moment, a gun roared and a bullet ploughed into the snow close to Hendrix's boot. Men were looming out of the gloom.

He shouted out, 'For God's sake, don't shoot. I'm

the railway man. I caught one of them outlaws, knocked him out!'

Men called to each other, then emerged from the darkness. 'You got one of them!' somebody asked.

'Sure. Here. See for yourself.' Hendrix gestured towards the unconscious man, and suddenly he was bustled aside as the men of the posse joined him, all peering down.

'Well, I be damned! Still wearing his mask.'

Men were stooping, dragging Grant to his feet, but Hendrix was not lingering to follow events. He was too busy fading into the gloom, rushing down-slope in the direction in which his own men had disappeared. His departure went unnoticed. The attention of the vigilantes was focused on their prisoner, dragging the mask from his face, slapping his cheeks to revive him, cursing him as goddamned trash that deserved the lynching he was going to get.

Between now and dawn, Grant, in agony from his broken jaw, would protest his innocence in vain, cursing the fact that none of the vigilantes recognized him as a railway man because in that gloomy night he had remained inconspicuous. Huddled in his coat and scarf, he had been forgotten as he lagged behind – and now, because he had been caught wearing an outlaw's bandanna, nobody gave him the chance to establish his true identity and explain what had happened. The fact was he hardly remembered himself, having been unconscious for most of the time. And one other thing became overwhelmingly evident: the vigilantes had been thwarted in their aim to capture the entire outlaw gang – thwarted by the darkness, the weather and circumstance. *But at least they had one man who would pay the penalty for his evil ways – or so they thought.*

FOUR

'If you read it in a book,' Doctor Brininstool remarked, 'you wouldn't believe it. An obvious example of the comatose.'

It was hours later in the surgery. For a moment the only sound was the bluster of wind hitting the windows.

Joe Evans, looked at the rise and fall of Grant's chest with amazed eyes. 'Surely he can't still be alive,' he gasped. 'Not after the hanging and all.'

'First time I've ever come across such a thing in my life, boy.'

Quite roughly Brininstool felt the neck of the man on his table. 'It's not broken,' he said. 'Just a bit of ligament tear. The trachea seems to be intact. But his jaw sure is a mess.'

Evans sighed with relief. 'Well I guess justice has been done, him still being alive. Must be God's will. I never figured he was guilty, never figured he deserved what they did to him.'

'Oh, the fact that he's breathing won't make much difference to him,' the doctor said. 'I'll soon dispatch

29

him to the next world, and he can sort matters out with the good Lord when he gets there.'

'You're not going to—'

'Oh, yes I am!' Brininstool turned to a side shelf and picked up a small surgical knife. 'I'll just open a vein. He'll quietly bleed to death and nobody'll be any the wiser.'

'Doctor Brininstool, sir,' Evans gasped, 'you can't do that. It's going against that oath you told me about. What was it? Didn't it say you must never take life but always try to save it. The hypocritical oath, wasn't it?'

'The Hippocratic oath,' Brininstool corrected, smiling at the boy's naïveté. 'There are times when the interests of medical science are more important than any oath.' He reached for a metal basin and placed it on the table. 'Could be a messy business, this. We don't want blood all over the place. You get ready to catch it as it drains off. There's another bowl on the side if you need it.'

He tested the sharpness of the blade with his thumb. He was seeking a suitable vein to open, when the bell from the outside door clanged an urgent twice.

'Damnation!' the doctor grunted. 'You go tell them they must come back later, that I'm busy.'

At that moment, the body on the table emitted a long moan, drawing their attention. Grant had opened his eyes, was staring at them. He tried to say something, but couldn't get the words past his bruised lips.

The boy was in a highly agitated state. 'You can't kill

him, just like that. It would be sinful.'

Brininstool snarled at his apprentice. 'Do as you're told or you'll be out of a job!'

'I won't be an accomplice to no crime,' Evans responded, his eyes stubborn and wild.

The doctor cursed, finding the vein he sought in Grant's arm, but suddenly the boy's voice came, level and determined.

'You put that knife aside, Doctor Brininstool, sir, or it'll be you who goes to your maker!'

The doctor turned, found himself gazing into the business end of his own Peacemaker, which Evans had grabbed from the dresser.

'I swear I'll shoot you dead,' the youngster cried, 'if you so much as place a finger on that poor helpless man. He's suffered enough.'

Both Brininstool and Evans started as the doorbell clanged again, but neither moved to answer it.

The doctor visibly relaxed. He placed his knife down upon the table and smiled. 'Come on, Joe,' he said softly. 'There's no cause for you and me to fall out. You just put that gun back on the dresser and we'll pretend the last few minutes never happened.'

'No sir!'

'In that case,' Brininstool said, 'there's something you'd better know. That gun's not loaded, never was. I'm a doctor, not a vigilante.'

The boy dropped his eyes to the gun in his hand, his eyes filled with dismay.

Brininstool stepped forward, rested his hand upon the Peacemaker's five-sided barrel. 'Just give it to me, boy.'

Evans's immediate reaction was to tug the gun away from the doctor's outstretched hand. It was sheer misfortune that his finger happened to be curled around the trigger and that the additional pressure caused the gun to blast off. The sound filled the room, had the windows rattling.

Evans recoiled in horror, dropping the gun. 'You said it weren't loaded.'

Outside at the front door, Mrs Fairfax had come to summon the doctor to her husband who had been nicked by a bullet during the fight with the outlaw gang. She had given the bell another impatient tug, and that was when she heard the unmistakable detonation of the shot. She had gasped in alarm. Surely the doctor hadn't shot one of his patients!

A moment later she was rushing down the street, slipping in the snow, heading for the cabin of Seth Fryer, chairman of the vigilantes. He must be informed immediately if there was lawlessness afoot. She banged on his door. Seth Fryer was sitting close to a glowing stove, writing down his vigilante report concerning the events of the previous twenty-four hours, at least those of which he was aware. Answering the hammering on his door, he saw the woman's alarmed expression.

'Gunshot,' she gasped. 'I heard a gunshot at Doc Brininstool's.'

'Steady, woman,' Fryer responded. 'Are you sure?'

'No mistake.' She nodded and he stood up. He reached for his gunbelt, strapped it around his waist, then took his hat and coat from his coat-stand and put them on. Within a minute, he was pacing through the snow, the woman stumbling in his wake, her curiosity having overtaken concerns as to the plight of her wounded husband.

At Brininstool's surgery light showed through the gaps in the curtains. Fryer peered through. He could see the doctor's table, but nothing was upon it, and further vision was restricted He wondered where Brininstool was working on the corpse. Accompanied by Mrs Fairfax, he went around to the front of the building and pulled the bell-cord, creating a considerable racket. When no response came, he tried again. Still nobody opened up.

Shaking his head impatiently, he turned. He still felt angry that he'd relinquished the body to the doctor, thus robbing him of the joy of gloating over it. 'We better check the rear of the building,' he grunted.

Mrs Fairfax nodded and followed along, drawing her shawl about her shoulders and saying, 'Dear me, I hope everything's all right.'

They found the back door of the surgery unlocked and Fryer led the way in. He saw Brininstool sitting in a chair, slumped forward.

He prodded Brininstool's shoulder. To his astonishment, the doctor slid from the chair on to the floor, doubled over like a child's rag doll. In so doing, he displayed his back, displayed the hole where a bullet had exited.

When Fryer pulled Brininstool's shoulders back, Mrs Fairfax screamed.

The doctor's shirtfront was blackened by a close-fired gunshot, the blood oozing darkly from the wound.

Soon it was staining the floor.

'Don't need no doctor to certify that he's a goner,' Seth Fryer remarked, inwardly resenting the fact that there had been a killing in which he'd not been involved.

FIVE

'You can't have done!' Mrs Anne Evans gasped, dropping the shirt she'd been sewing into the lap of her homespun apron. She was an attractive forty-year-old woman with a dignified manner. Her red hair was pulled back tight and coiled in a Psyche knot on the nape of her neck.

In the parlour of the small house off Main Street, young Joe Evans was perched, ashen-faced, on a rocking-chair. 'I did, Ma. As he tried to grab the gun, it went off. Shot him through the chest. He sort of tottered off, slumped into a chair and when I checked him, he was real dead.'

For a moment they sat in stunned silence.

'But you didn't mean to kill him?' Kathryn Evans, Joe's twin sister, eventually asked.

Both women gazed at him with horrified expressions, waiting for his answer.

'No,' he said.

By the fireside, Grant was slumped on a heavy-tufted black sofa. He had little recollection of the day's tragedies, being now mainly concerned with his awful stiff neck and the pain that throbbed through his jaw.

He could vaguely recall how the boy had half-carried him, half-dragged him, out of the doctor's surgery via the back entrance. How they had stumbled down the deserted street through thickly falling snow, how finally they had been admitted into a house where a log fire brought welcome warmth. He felt weak, unable to do anything but sprawl on the sofa where he'd been placed.

Both women were highly agitated by Joe's words, but Kathryn stepped across and gazed at Grant. Like her kinfolk, her hair was the colour of a tawny, autumn leaf. She had large, greenish eyes, with eyelashes like her hair. Her features were those of her twin brother, though in a feminine way.

Her face was full of concern. 'You poor fella,' she murmured. 'That jaw of yours looks real ugly. Don't try to speak. It'll hurt too much.'

He managed a nod, feeling her compassion was well placed.

'I'll make him some gruel,' Mrs Evans said, coming to her feet. 'He needs something to fortify him.'

'Ma,' Joe said, 'once they find the doctor, they're bound to come looking for me.'

'Then you'll have to explain how it was an accident,' his mother consoled him, but the frightened look in his eyes remained.

'Nobody'll believe me. Seth Fryer's blind to all reason. We've got to get away.'

'You can't go out in this weather,' Mrs Evans protested, 'not the way you are.'

'I'll take him,' Joe said. 'I'll get a horse from the stable and we'll ride double. It's no more than twenty miles to Catto.'

'And you'll probably sink in some snowdrift,' his twin sister cut in.

'That'll be better,' the boy argued, 'than being lynched by Seth Fryer and his mob.'

'How will they know it was you who did the shooting?' Kathryn asked. She was a girl who spoke her thoughts in a forthright manner.

Joe's eyes were melancholy. He gestured towards Grant. 'Well, it must've been him or me, weren't nobody else there. And they probably still think he's a corpse.'

Mrs Evans shrugged her shoulders with exasperation. 'Well not before we get something inside you, otherwise you'll never stand up to the cold.' She bustled away to her stove, poked it into life and set a skillet to simmer. Within five minutes she was ladling gruel into bowls, and Katherine found a spoon and was soon feeding Grant as if he'd been a toddler.

'Open wider,' she murmured, 'let it go down slowly.'

He groaned, but he felt the comforting liquid flow into his mouth and trickle down his throat. The intense way she attended to him warmed him. Had it not been for his pain, he would have enjoyed her nearness, even her bossy-boots manner.

Joe, too, was eating, realizing that he would need strength for what lay ahead. As he chewed, he stood close to the window, parting the curtain a crack, gazing out into the snowy street. Suddenly he straightened his spine, let the curtain drop back.

'He's coming, Ma! Seth Fryer!'

'Well, he won't be having you, Joe,' his mother said. 'You finish eating.'

The boy shrank from the window, visibly shaken, but Anne Evans's face had taken on a determined look. She stood waiting, hardly flinching when there was a heavy pounding on the door. She paused for a time equivalent to five breaths, then she calmly raised the latch and drew open the door a fraction to confront the chairman of the vigilantes. His giant bulk was coated with snow.

'I'm looking for Joe?' he stated.

'Well, he's not here,' she lied convincingly. 'I've not seen hide nor hair of him since he left with Doctor Brininstool last night.'

Fryer growled his disappointment. 'Well, Doctor Brininstool is dead, shot with his own gun—'

'Dead!' Anne Evans gasped, glad that she had once had dreams of becoming an actress. 'I can't believe it.'

'It's true. And the corpse he was intent on slicing up has disappeared. The boy must know what happened. That's why I need to speak to him. Anne, can I come in a moment? It's cold standing here.'

Anne Evans assumed a look of horror. 'Seth Fryer,' she said, 'you're like a snowman. You'll flood my floor once you get near a fire.'

He growled in exasperation. 'Well, you let me know as soon as the boy shows up. Reckon he has a few questions to answer.'

'I sure will,' she said.

'Anne,' he said earnestly, 'you wouldn't be telling me lies, would you, not knowing the way we feel for each other?'

She gave her head a firm shake, her lips pursed.

He hesitated, then waved his arm in farewell gesture.

Anne Evans closed the door and pressed her back against it. She had gone as white as alabaster. She had never told so many lies in her entire life.

To her surprise, Grant had somehow struggled to his feet and Kathryn was helping him put his coat on. Joe, too, was preparing to leave.

'I'm sorry, Ma,' he said, 'making you lie for me. I've got to get away before Seth Fryer comes back. We can't stay here.'

'You be careful, Joe,' she said. 'You keep hidden till we can work something out.' She turned to Grant as his Texas drawl came in a painful whisper.

'I'm grateful to you, ma'am. I'm sorry I got you into all this trouble.'

She nodded and said, 'If you're a friend of Joe's, that's good enough for us. God's will be done.'

'Amen,' Kathryn commented, her eyes seeming unwilling to relinquish their hold on Grant.

Joe peered at Grant's swollen jaw. 'Let me bind that for you,' he said, 'wrap a scarf around. At least that'll keep it in place.'

Soon Grant was suffering the pain as the boy tied a scarf about his head and knotted it firmly.

Suddenly an impish light came into Kathryn's eyes. 'Better not get tired and yawn. The pain'd kill you.'

Anne Evans frowned at her daughter and said, 'Now's not the time for jokes, Kath.'

Five minutes later, Grant and the boy left the house by the back door. Swaying on his feet, Grant waited in a shadowy side-alley while Joe went to the stable and returned with a sorrel horse, ready saddled. The two of them mounted the beast's broad back, Grant clinging on behind, and a moment later they were leaving town, riding out into the murk. By the time they had gone a hard-won mile, heavy darkness had descended and the wind bore into them. They were progressing at a snail's pace, the sorrel was already labouring, and freezing snow was making breathing a problem. Joe turned his head, fighting to make his voice heard above the roar of the gale.

'Guess we can't go no further in this,' he shouted, turning his face away from the wind. 'Best hole up till it lessens. At least nobody'll be out hunting for us in this weather.'

Grant raised his hand in agreement, but inwardly he was not so sure. He'd never encountered a meaner individual than Seth Fryer. He wondered if the chairman of the vigilantes had discovered that the man he'd strung up was still breathing. If he did, he'd sure as hell be taking up his trail. And even if hadn't reached that conclusion, he was bound to be searching for the boy.

None the less, in the blind gut of this gale, there was no arguing. They dismounted and found shelter in a small copse.

Grant knew that he owed Joe Evans a great debt. And now the boy was in serious trouble because of him, and this grieved him. As they awaited the heartless dawn, Joe told him how Brininstool had been shot – a terrible accident, but had it not occurred, there was no doubt that Grant would have died and his skull been opened up. 'Figure there was only one thing I wanted to be, ever since I was a kid. A doctor like Brininstool. He taught me a lot, but I guess he went too far when he said he'd open your vein, let you die.

He said that gun wasn't loaded and I believed him.'

The Texan placed an understanding hand on the boy's shoulder.

In the eight years he had tended his flock, not one person had ever suspected that as well as being an ordained priest, the Reverend Benjamin Hendrix had another string to his bow – that of outlaw. Now he sat in his office working on his Sunday sermon. Five years back, he'd salvaged the walls and roof of the church from a nearby ghost town, transported them to Barclay and had a church erected. It was easy to get pews and pulpit made cheaply by the local carpenter. The bell, conveyed from Miles City at some expense, had been hoisted into the steeple, its rope hanging down near the entrance of the church. Over the years he'd imbued in the place a Gothic style with arched windows and steeply gabled roof. Hendrix preached on the sins of the flesh, on greed and jealousy, and on how evil it was to covet another man's property. He would preach in his gentle, understanding way, and this never conveyed any other sentiment than sincerity. He smiled to himself. He had built up a reputation as a kindly pastor, a person any man or woman could call upon if they needed help, spiritual or otherwise. His mouth constantly wore a benign smile and his manner was always that of profound courtesy. Few people noticed that his smile never reached his eyes.

He was not one of Seth Fryer's vigilantes, being a man of the cloth. He always claimed he was in the business of saving souls, not stringing them up, and that was why he was away so much, attending theology college, on gospel missions and devoting himself single-mind-edly to the Lord's work.

Since his teenage years, he'd harboured a genuine interest in spiritual matters and faith in the Lord, and it had only seemed natural that he should study at theology college in his hometown of Philadelphia. He had passed with flying colours, impressing his mentors to such an extent that he finished top of his class. He could have chosen a prestigious stipend in the East, but there was something about the Far West that had intrigued him. It was here, he maintained, that true sinners existed. In consequence he was appointed to the new stipend in Barclay where he soon gained considerable respect. But gradually, over the years, he became restless, finding a darker and even more compulsive side to his character. He grew tired of his adopted manner of meekness and yearned for some more adventurous activity.

His interest was aroused when, one dark winter night five years back, a wounded outlaw had come to his church begging sanctuary. Hendrix was intrigued, took the man in, treated his wound, hid and fed him. He learned that this stranger was a man called Frank Clayton and that he was wanted in several states on charges of robbery. The two struck up a relationship, found that deep down their spirits bore remarkable similarity. At first Hendrix had harboured dreams of converting this man to godly ways. But a strange thing had happened. By the time Clayton was fit enough to resume his normal life, it was he who had done the converting, convincing the reverend how rewarding a life of crime could be – and how well a man of the cloth was placed to pick up news of profitable shipments of wealth or institutions where gold was stored.

Clayton had said that he could supply the manpower if Hendrix would use his undoubted mental ability and power over the minds of other men to achieve gains beyond their wildest dreams. After all, nobody would suspect that a seemingly devout priest was behind acts of felony.

Hendrix had constantly been aware of the dilapidated state of his church, frequently looked upon it as an insult to the Lord. Perhaps divine power had sent this man to him, offering a means of building an establishment worthy of not only the Lord, but of his own achievements in the field of theology.

The two men drew up plans. Certainly the recovered Frank Clayton left Barclay with a greater respect for the Lord, but he, in turn, left behind a reverend who saw a future full of opportunity, his twisted mind convinced that such activity rested comfortably within his ordained path.

He thus assumed two personalities, having recently read Robert Louis Stevenson's novel *Dr Jekyll and Mr Hyde*, and finding in the doctor's personality something akin to his own. He was soon undertaking criminal deeds, enjoying the contrast between the meek Benjamin Hendrix and the hardened outlaw leader that he became.

Never once, when undertaking the crimes of his other life, had Hendrix's face been exposed other than to his close associates. But on the previous night, the railwayman had snatched away his mask, got a glimpse of his features. Admittedly, Hendrix had switched attention away from himself by donning the railroad cap, but he was sure his ruse of pretending that the unconscious man was an outlaw would soon be tumbled to. Thereafter folks, and especially Seth Fryer, would start putting two and two together. One thing was certain, he couldn't afford to let anybody who might recognize him remain in the land of the living.

He rose from his desk and was soon tolling the church bell, inviting his parishioners to evening service, but meanwhile his brain was working on less godly matters, attempting to form a strategy.

SIX

'Anne!' Seth Fryer's beak-nosed face was working with fury. 'I've spoken to the hostler, and he said the boy came out the back of this house and took his horse from the stable. He said there was another fella waiting for him, seemed kinda unsteady on his feet and that they headed out o' town, riding double. You had no right to tell me a pack o' lies!'

This time he had barged right into the parlour of the Evans house, not caring that thawing snow was dripping from his coat, forming a puddle on the hard-scrubbed floor.

Anne Evans made no response, just stood looking at him, her eyes wide with resentment. Beside her was a heap of laundry, which she took in, together with needlework, to earn a living.

'I know the boy's guilty of something, maybe of killing poor Doctor Brininstool and making off with that corpse, though God knows what he intends to do with it. Why did you tell me them lies?'

'You'd know why,' she said, 'if you'd ever been a true parent. If you had an ounce of love in your soul.'

He scoffed at her words. 'Well, I can tell you something. That boy ain't gonna make a fool of me. I'll find him and he'll have to face justice.'

'Justice,' she snapped. 'You don't know the meaning of the word. The only justice you dispense is at the end of a rope, guilty or not!'

'I'll make you regret what you're saying, Anne Evans. I'll catch that boy, and he'll have to tell the truth or face the consequences, or most likely both. You mark my words!'

'Whatever happened,' Anne Evans countered, 'was an accident. You'd learn far more about the truth if you didn't go around terrorizing everybody.'

He scowled at her, then turned on his heel, pulled open the door and stepped out into the street, ducking his head as he went, his profane muttering snatched away by the wind.

Behind him, Anne Evans's show of bravado left her, and she was suddenly tearful and burying her face in her apron. Her daughter Kathryn slipped a comforting arm about her shoulders. They both felt helpless, and utterly dismayed by events.

That night there were only a dozen worshippers who braved the weather to attend church. They all prayed that the weather would improve. After the service, Seth Fryer was the last to leave, lingering back for a word with the minister.

'Reverend,' he said, 'I know you're always telling us about Christ rising from the dead, but have you ever known normal folk to do it?'

The Reverend Benjamin Hendrix shook his head. 'No, can't say I have. Why do you ask?'

'Well, you probably heard how we lynched that outlaw and Doctor Brininstool took possession of the body to carry out medical research.'

Hendrix gave a glum nod. 'I heard. And now poor Doc Brininstool has gone to the after-life himself, shot down in his own surgery. Who could've done such a thing?'

The reverend's brain was ticking over fast. So a man had been lynched. That must be the fellow whom he'd knocked out and draped in his calico mask. He felt inwardly pleased. Could be Fryer and his posse had saved him the job of killing the man himself, eased him the worry of having somebody walking around who could recognize him. But then a doubt clouded his mind.

'You're not saying,' he said, 'that Brininstool has risen from the dead? I'm supposed to be conducting the funeral just as soon as the ground can be dug.'

'No, it ain't Brininstool. He'll be ready for burying just as soon as you are. It's the other fella, the one we strung up. I'm damned sure it's him who's left town with young Joe Evans.'

'How can it be!' The reverend's face was aghast.

'Must be some miracle,' Fryer grunted. 'You believe in miracles don't you, reverend?'

'Sure I do. Christ was crucified and was resurrected, but I can't see how it could happen to a common outlaw.'

'Well, I know one thing. The two of them ain't gonna get far in this weather, especially if one of them's nothing more than a spirit. I figure they must be heading for Catto and come morning, I'll be takin' up their trail.

47

Nobody's gonna make a fool out o' Seth Fryer.'

The reverend came to a sudden decision. 'I'll come with you. Some spiritual guidance may be needed.'

'That's good o' you,' Fryer nodded. 'We'll ride out first thing tomorrow mornin'. Meanwhile you pray the weather will be better.'

After the chairman of the vigilantes had left, hunching his shoulders against the blizzard, the Reverend Benjamin Hendrix locked up the church. He couldn't imagine how that railroad man had survived the lynching, but he was determined he wouldn't survive much longer. Miracles wouldn't stretch that far.

SEVEN

Lynching maybe had its downside, but at this moment Grant figured that having his jaw fixed rigid, with thread passed between each tooth, was ten times worse. It was a torturous experience. A wave of panic surged through him. He felt he was somehow trapped inside his own head, that his tongue was like an angry snake, darting this way and that, unable to escape from its cage. Not that Doctor Carter hadn't done his utmost to calm his patient. He'd carried out a precise job with all the gentleness and expertise he could muster, but he was dealing with a fracture of the lower jaw and just breathing near it was enough to have poor Grant writhing with pain. Even half a bottle of prime whiskey hadn't subdued him.

He was sprawled in the armchair in the doctor's surgery in Catto, where young Joe Evans had somehow delivered him. The hours in the blizzard had been purgatory, and they had huddled together for body warmth, but come daylight they had managed to forge onward through the snow, praying that the foul weather would discourage any would-be pursuers.

Now, Carter nodded with satisfaction. He was an

overweight man with the flesh under his chin compressed by his starched collar, but he carried out his work with surprising dexterity. He was particularly pleased in that he knew he would get paid for his efforts in hard cash. For his work, in this town of Catto, he so often had to accept payment in kind. Sometimes he got nothing.

Joe Evans was also in the room, anxious to help this man whom fate had treated so badly over the past days, and equally aware of his own precarious circumstances. Concern had him running his thin hand through his red hair. Several times he paced across to the window and peered out, half expecting to see Seth Fryer and his posse riding up the street, hunting the killer of Doc Brininstool. He shuddered, but at the moment there was no sign of them.

Grant's eyes were still wild from the ordeal he'd passed through. He heard the doctor's words through a haze of inebriation. 'Make sure that jaw stays closed for two, maybe three months and then keep it out of trouble. I've chipped a gap between the front teeth so you can get a straw through. You got to wash your mouth out twice a day. Remember, no solid food. It'll be liquid, good rich gruel, until I cut this thread away. Understand, young man?'

Grant managed the slightest nod, wincing at the pain it caused.

'Yes, it's your neck that looks downright bad,' the doctor continued. 'Terrible bruising you got there. It's almost as if you were . . . lynched.'

'He was,' Joe Evans commented. He'd been watching, fascinated by Carter's skills, wondering if he might find employment as his assistant once certain troubles had been cleared up.

'He was lynched?' The doctor emitted a grim laugh. He enjoyed a good joke, and he never made a habit of probing too deeply into the causes of men's injuries. It just didn't pay with so many carrying guilty secrets in their pasts, especially if they were paying up front.

Grant rested for a couple of hours in the room behind the surgery, Joe Evans watching over him like an attentive nurse. Eventually the Texan sat up and nodded to his companion, indicating he was fit enough to move on. Movement brought pangs of pain lancing through his jaw but he was in no condition to complain. Despite his traumatic experiences, he still had money in his pocket. He paid the doctor, then he and Joe made their way out into Catto's main street. The weather remained bitterly cold, but the snow had eased off. Stores were open and folks were on the sidewalks.

Grant and Joe Evans went warily, glancing about for sign that Fryer might be waiting to jump out at them, but they reached Grant's lodgings on Colby Street without trouble and a moment later were in the warm parlour of Mrs Tolly, a cheerful, rotund landlady in a red apron, who was deeply concerned at Grant's predicament. She promised that she would ensure he was served with the tastiest of gruels and other liquids until his jaw healed.

Soon, she had made up an extra bed for Joe in Grant's room. After a hot meal, spooned, in the railwayman's case, through the gap drilled between his front teeth, the two lodgers took to their beds, glad enough for rest.

Grant's mind meandered, as so often, through memories of his time with Josephine and of the awful days when diphtheria had caught her. Doctors had applied a solution of nitrate of silver to her throat, but all in vain. She had died in his arms, her sad and jaundiced eyes, so recently sparkling with merriment, pleading for a relief he was unable to give.

He pondered on other matters, trying to convince himself that the recent events had all been a nightmare. But he lay, feeling the throb of pain through his neck and jaw, and knew that the horror could not be discarded so easily.

Presently he slept but eventually pain awoke him and he lay hearing the gentle rasp of Joe's breathing. More than ever, he was conscious of how much he owed to his companion. They were both in an incredible mess. Fryer was not the sort of man to give up easily and he would not listen to reason. Once he set his mind on justice being done, the rope was the only way forward. With his jaw fastened tight, Grant would have even less chance of arguing his case. He'd already tried once, but that had brought him no joy – and the death of Doctor Brininstool would only worsen the case for both him and the boy.

Grant knew that he would have to report to his boss at the railroad and make sure that the truth of his identity and his actions prior to the misunderstanding were somehow made absolutely clear to Fryer. But he was uncertain how to help Joe. Only he knew that the bullet that had killed Doctor Brininstool had been discharged in error. But there was no finesse about law as far as the vigilantes were concerned. A killing was a killing in their eyes, and the punishment would come with brutal swiftness once they laid hands on the perpetrator.

Grant tried to form a plan, but his mind seemed devoid of any ideas and he eventually lapsed into troubled sleep again.

He was wakened, late next morning, by the shunting of wagons from the railroad depot behind the house. He knew he must contact his boss as soon as possible. He became aware that Joe Evans was standing near the window, peering down the street. His body had become rigid with tenseness.

'Fryer's just ridden into town,' he gasped. 'There's another fella with him – looks like the reverend from the church in Barclay! They've hitched their horses outside the saloon. Fryer's gone in.'

Grant could do nothing but swallow hard. He wondered if Fryer might come asking for him, but then he recalled that the vigilante leader did not know his identity. To him, he was an outlaw who, by all the laws of nature, should be dead. The best thing he and Joe could do was to stay hidden – but then another concern troubled him. There was somebody who might give Fryer a clue as to their presence, and that was Doctor Carter.

'Why should the Reverend Hendrix be riding with Fryer?' Evans murmured.

Grant shook his head, grimacing at the pain it caused his neck, and then another possibility occurred to him. Maybe somebody had noticed him and the boy riding into town, doubled up on the one horse. Somebody might well put two and two together and point the way to Mrs Tolly's lodging house.

*

As the chairman of the vigilantes and the minister had ridden from Barclay along the snowy trail, the weather had relented. Thin sunlight was piercing the clouds, finding particles of ice to glint upon. Hendrix had paid little attention to the stark beauty of the terrain, because his thoughts were dwelling on certain tasks he considered of paramount importance. Firstly, the railwayman must be found and shot down. Hendrix wouldn't rest while there was somebody around who would know his face and subsequently blow his ruse to bits. He realized, being a minister of religion, that he could not actually do the shooting himself, that was if anybody else was watching. So he had to string along with Fryer who, he hoped, would do the dirty work for him.

As for Seth Fryer, Hendrix hated the giant's guts, but for the present he would conceal his feelings. The chairman of the vigilantes was his arch enemy, and the funny thing about it was that Fryer didn't associate him with outlaw activity. Hendrix would let him remain in ignorance – right up until the time he would kill him himself. The vigilantes were a thorn in the side of the outlaws, and Fryer would have no compunction in stringing up anybody he suspected was a member of the gang. He could not be allowed to continue his violence in the name of law and order.

And so, here were two men, each wishing violence on the other, though only one of them knew it.

As they approached Catto, it was early afternoon. They passed a group of railroad workers, armed with their tools, moving in the opposite direction. Obviously they were going to repair the damaged track, little suspecting that the pious-looking minister they passed was at the root of the trouble. Hendrix smiled to himself, then frowned as he recalled that the operation to rob the train had gone awry. Had matters proceeded as intended, he would be a rich man now.

Riding into Main Street, Hendrix's attention was drawn to a scurry of activity outside the local bank. Under armed guard, boxes of cash were being unloaded from a security wagon and carried into the bank. Hendrix smiled. He had long held dreams of robbing a bank. Now, with the railroad job having gone awry, he earmarked bank robbery for his next job. Firstly he would have to do some planning, but before that, there were other matters to attend to.

'You wait here, Reverend,' Seth Fryer muttered as they reined in their horses outside the saloon. 'Keep your eyes peeled for any sight of our friends. I'll make a few enquiries inside.' He dropped from his saddle and fastened his horse to the hitch rail.

Hendrix nodded. He could have done with some liquid refreshment himself, but, as a reverend, it would not do for him to frequent a saloon.

Seth Fryer shouldered his way through the batwings. The bar-room was pretty quiet at this time of day, but he found a man behind the bar, polishing glasses. Fryer ordered a whiskey and as the man slid a bottle and glass across the counter to him, he hoisted his great body on to a stool.

'I'm looking for some friends of mine,' he said. 'Wonder if you've seen any strangers ride into town.'

'Not in this weather,' the barman grunted. 'Not

many folks have been travelling around in all this snow.'

Fryer nodded, uncorking the bottle and pouring himself a stiff tot. 'You'd have noticed my friends if you'd seen them,' he said. 'Two fellows riding on the one horse. One of them looking more dead than alive, I guess.'

The barman's expression had changed, but he didn't like giving out information to a man he didn't know. 'You say you're a friend of theirs?'

Fryer sipped his liquor. 'Sure I am. And they're in desperate need of some help. Me and the reverend have come over from Barclay to lend them a hand.'

The man behind the bar obviously knew something, but still he hesitated. It was only when Fryer slipped a silver dollar across the counter that his reluctance to communicate melted away.

'Well, don't let on I told you,' he said. 'But sure I saw two men on one horse ride into town. It was yesterday. One of them looked no more than a boy.'

'Where are they now?' Fryer asked, excitement glinting from his deep-set eyes.

The other man shook his head. 'Don't rightly know, but if you ask at Doc Carter's, he might be able to tell you. You'll find his surgery four blocks down the street.'

Fryer nodded his thanks, threw back his whiskey and rejoined Hendrix outside. He told him what he had learned. 'Only trouble is,' he said, 'the doc may be unwilling to tell us anything.'

'Not if a reverend asks him,' Hendrix grunted.

'I'll wait in the saloon while you make a few enquiries, then.'

Hendrix touched his clerical hat in acknowledgement and rode off down the street. He easily found the sign marked JOSEPH CARTER, PRACTITIONER OF MEDICINE. To his disappointment, the doctor was away seeing to a patient, but a lady who was probably his wife was quite taken with the idea of helping a minister of the church with his charitable duties.

'Your friends are lodging at Mrs Tolly's. One of them had a broken jaw. The other was a young boy. I'm sure they'll be real pleased for a little spiritual help. You'll find the lodging house, first turning on the left in Colby Street. You can't miss it.'

Hendrix touched the brim of his hat and murmured, 'I'm right grateful to you. God be with you, ma'am.'

Fryer was waiting for him on the sidewalk outside the saloon. He received the information with an eager nod and unbuttoned his coat so that his gun was within easy reach. 'Well done, Reverend. Now we got some work to do.'

A moment later the two men turned their horses into Colby Street.

EIGHT

Grant glanced at his companion and then indicated with a nod of his head that it would be wise to leave by the back way of the house. He felt he must get to the railroad office, even board a train if they could. He was still feeling light-headed from his harrowing experiences, but they went down the stairs and as they did so, there was a thumping on the front door. Mrs Tolly, a small, plump pigeon of a woman, appeared from her kitchen, an anxious expression on her face. She was not aware of the exact nature of the trouble, but her affection for Grant had always been considerable.

'Do you want me to answer?' she asked as the thumping sounded again, this time more insistent.

Grant shook his head and through his clenched teeth, said, 'Not for a minute. Give us time to get away . . . and thank you.'

She said, 'Be careful. Come back when you can.'

They went through the kitchen, and Joe followed Grant out through the back door into the yard outside. Clouds had come up, bringing a fresh flurry of snow, and the light was melting into early dusk.

The railroad depot was about 150 yards ahead of

them, across rough scrub ground, but as they hurried towards it, a voice cried out, 'Stay where you are! Or I'll fire!'

'Keep running,' Joe panted out. 'It's Fryer. Must've come round the side of the house.'

Grant nodded, but as the two tore their way through the scrubby grass, Fryer's big Dragoon boomed. Grant drew up, twisted round, and gasped in horror. The boy was sprawled on the ground. Oblivious to his own safety, Grant dropped to his knees and then cried out in anguish. Joe Evans was dead, half his head blown off.

Grant saw Seth Fryer stumbling towards him, his revolver raised. The vigilante fired, the bullet whining past Grant's ear. Now it was Grant's turn. Kneeling as he was beside the boy, his hand closed over a rock. Hatred for Fryer gave him strength, and he hurled the rock with all his power, striking the giant in his stomach. He howled with pain, doubled over, dropping his weapon.

Grant turned his back on him, stooped over the boy, pleading that his first impression of the injury had been wrong. But not all the pleading in the world would change matters. Joe Evans, a gallant ally to the end, was beyond help, this side of Heaven anyway. The boy had given his life for Grant and despair blurred the Texan's eyes.

Grant heard Fryer's cursing and, turning, he saw him scrambling to retrieve his gun. Grant took a deep shuddering breath and stumbled onward towards the railroad, but at the same time he was increasingly aware of his own weakness. He was like a wounded beast soon to be run down by its predator. He realized that the minister must have been at the front of the house, banging

59

on the door, while Fryer had come round to the back, the speed of their escape initially preventing the vigilante from barring their way.

Now, Grant heard voices raised, shouting at him to come back. Glancing over his shoulder, he could see that Fryer had been joined by the minister and the two of them were coming in pursuit of him. Again, a shot sounded and Grant heard the *whizz* of lead through the cold air. If they fired again, as they got closer, he might not be so lucky. But the railroad buildings were looming ahead, showing darkly against the sky. A freight train was standing in the depot, about to depart and the hope it afforded somehow gave the Texan new determination.

Reaching the train, he saw an open door on one of the freight cars. He grasped up and hauled himself into its gloomy interior. The car was empty, apart from a mass of straw, and he contemplated diving into it and hiding himself, but he realized that his actions would have been seen by his pursuers and the car would be a trap. In consequence, he slid open the door on the far side and half-fell, half-jumped out. He fell heavily but, ignoring pain, forced himself to his feet. He stumbled along the side of the train and then, knowing he would be a clear target, he ducked in between the wheels and lay on the sleepers, his breath heaving. He could still hear Fryer's voice. He was shouting like a maniac. He knew the vigilante would have no compunction in shooting him dead, just the same way as he had poor Joe, but he knew that the great Dragoon was not quickly reloaded.

Grant goaded his weakening limbs into renewed

effort. He had no idea what he could do to escape his enemies. He gazed out between the wheels, but the snow was coming down thickly, the light was dimmer and he could see little. He dragged himself along the track towards the head of the train, bruising his knees on the sleepers and the rocks between them. Fryer's voice had quieted. No doubt he was searching the straw in the wagon but he would soon discover that he was wasting his time.

Tension was running through the cars, couplings complaining as they took up the strain. The locomotive was easing forward. Grant took a deep breath, dodging out through the suddenly revolving wheels, feeling one brush against his leg. He realized he was just behind the wood tender. He hurled himself onward, aware of the increasing speed of the train and that he was racing against it. He overtook the coupling and reached the cab of the locomotive. He gazed up into the surprised face of the driver, illuminated in orange light from the glowing firebox. It was the Swede Hugo Eriksson – and thankfully he recognized him. He raised his arms and Eriksson, joined by his fireman, dragged him on to the footplate and into the cab.

Seth Fryer cursed as he finished kicking through the straw, his Dragoon held at the ready. He realized that he had been tricked, added to which his guts pained him. As the train was rumbling into motion, he jumped clear of the car, exiting the same way as Grant must have done. He glanced up and down the track, cursing again as he failed to see the fugitive in the failing light. He had no idea whether he had remained on the train or had escaped into the scrubland beyond.

Fryer felt his pain increasing. He figured he had some internal injury. He would have to get to the doctor in Catto.

With the train gone, he was joined by a disgruntled Hendrix, one dwarfing the other. The two stood together on the windswept railroad track, gazing at the rear lantern of the train as it disappeared into the gloom.

'I guess he's given us the slip, Reverend,' Fryer grunted sourly.

'There'll be another time,' Hendrix retorted. 'We'll find him and shoot him down like he deserves.'

Fryer gave Hendrix an odd look. 'I never heard you talk so tough before, Reverend.'

NINE

Anne Evans was slumped down in a chair, her face buried in her hands. Her daughter stood alongside, her eyes red with weeping.

Seth Fryer, and Hendrix looking pious in his clerical hat and coat, had paid her a visit and were standing in the parlour of the house, waiting and seemingly respectful as Anne and Kathryn absorbed the news that Joe was dead.

'We brought your son's body back,' the reverend said in a gentle voice. 'It's in the mortuary. You can go and see him if you wish, pay your respects. I've already said prayers for him.'

'You say he was shot in the head?' Kathryn asked, her voice scarcely more than a trembling whisper. News of her twin's death was like having half her soul torn out.

Seth Fryer nodded gravely. 'He and that other fella were running off. I called to them to wait, that we'd come to help them.'

'Then what happened?' Mrs Evans prompted, raising her tear-filled eyes.

Fryer coughed awkwardly, then said, 'Well, they didn't stop, so I called again. This time the fella with Joe did stop, and he seemed to have some sort of argument with Joe. Then he seemed to lose his temper completely, snatched a gun out, took aim and shot poor Joe.'

'It must've been an accident?' Kathryn Evans gasped.

'No,' Fryer replied. 'It was cold-blooded killing.'

'Oh God!' Mrs Evans sobbed. 'I just can't believe it.'

'Mr Fryer can only tell you what he saw, Mrs Evans,' Hendrix murmured. 'The one consolation is that he died straight away, didn't suffer any pain. Now, he's in the good hands of the Lord.'

Kathryn tried to speak, but she was too distraught. Joe dead, shot down by the man they had helped. It seemed unbelievable.

'You must remember,' Fryer said, 'that the man with Joe was a vicious criminal. He should've died by lynching, but he somehow escaped.'

Anne Evans stood up. 'If he was killed intentionally, you'll catch his murderer, won't you? I want you to promise he'll get the justice he deserves.'

'I promise that, Anne,' Seth Fryer said. 'I truly do, so help me God!'

Later that day, mother and daughter went to the town mortuary to see Joe. He lay on a slab. The undertaker had wrapped his head in a bandage because, he said, it would only make them feel bad to see it.

Hendrix had accompanied them, saying a few soothing prayers over the body. He enjoyed playing the part of a supportive priest, even at times felt that the Lord was guiding him.

'We'll get Joe buried as soon as we can,' the undertaker explained in his soft voice, 'but at present the ground's too hard to dig the grave. You can be assured he'll rest peacefully here until we can arrange the proper funeral.'

Anne Evans hardly seemed to hear him. She remembered that Joe had introduced his companion as Grant. If Grant had killed her son, then she would not rest until he faced justice.

The Reverend Benjamin Hendrix was not a happy man. He had set his mind on Seth Fryer's carrying out the execution of the railwayman, but his faith had been misplaced. It seemed that, next time, the minister would have to do the work himself. He was determined more than ever that the man who had seen his face, could connect him to the attempted railroad robbery, must not survive to create further trouble.

Meanwhile, he had something else on his mind. Robbing a bank. Maybe the job would be easier than robbing the train had proved to be. He would have to plan carefully. Firstly, he must destroy Grant Mayo, then he would do the bank job. In his mind, these tasks left no room for error.

Seth Fryer was in a foul mood over the next few days. His bruised stomach was downright sore, though the doctor in Catto had assured him it was nothing serious and had given him some pills. But it was the knowledge that he had been outwitted by the man he had tried to hang that hurt him the most. Fryer had been made to look a fool, but at least he had thwarted the train robbery. The rail company should be grateful for that.

He tried to make some sense out of what had

happened. He had made enquiries at the Catto rail depot and discovered that a man called Grant Mayo had disappeared. With great reluctance, Fryer eventually concluded that Mayo was the man he had tried to hang, and that there had been some confusion in the darkness over the railwayman's identity. Mayo had argued that he wasn't a member of the outlaw gang, but Fryer had been in no mood to listen to his seemingly false claims, knowing that a condemned man will say anything to escape the rope. Now Fryer had to face the fact that he might have been telling the truth. Incredibly the man had survived the lynching, and must have escaped with the aid of the boy Evans. If this was a fact, Evans had deserved the fate he had received, especially as either he or the surviving 'corpse' had assuredly murdered Doctor Brininstool.

But Fryer decided to play a crafty game. He spread no word regarding the death of the boy and his own false claim that Mayo had committed the murder. He didn't want any public-spirited individual arresting the railway man, bringing him in to stand trial. That way, the truth would leak out. Fryer was convinced there had been no outside witnesses of the boy's shooting, and he decided to bide his time.

Now Anne Evans would believe that Mayo had been responsible, and so would suffer her remorse at helping such a wicked man in the first place.

But the following day, Fryer decided to play his hand in a different way. When Anne Evans answered the knock on her door, she was startled to be confronted by the vigilante's intimidating presence. This time she could find no excuse to prevent him from entering. She was garbed in heavy black, her tearful face was creased with lines of grief at losing her son.

Fryer saw his chance, put his arm around Anne's shoulder, attempting to console her and she did not repel him, feeling that she had no strength.

In that instant, feeling her soft body against his, an excited reminiscence went through him. She had always known how he felt about her, had always fobbed him off, but suddenly now she gave vent to her emotions, her tears spilling on to his shirt front, and he realized that the pleasure this caused him went far beyond that of simply consoling her, awakened in him a passion his ugliness had so often prevented him from fulfilling. It brought a roaring to his ears, but he fought it back as he heard footsteps on the stairs and Kathryn entered the room.

Now was not the time, but he sensed that his chance would surely come.

TEN

Despite his misfortunes, Grant knew that luck had favoured him. Finding his Swedish friend Hugo Eriksson on the footplate of the departing train that night had been akin to divine intervention. Grant had slumped on the floor of the locomotive cab, unable to raise his voice in competition with the thunder of the rails and firebox, unable to convey the reasons for his frantic flight, but Hugo Eriksson sensed that his need was desperate, and as a fellow railwayman he did not stint in giving help.

Grant had not recalled very much as the train drew him away from his enemies, forging a passage of escape through the encroaching darkness and storm, had not recalled anything beyond the black grief inside him concerning the death of Joe Evans.

Later, his senses focused on the man who had gunned the boy down – Seth Fryer. The vigilante was using the shield of the law to satisfy his psychopathic instinct to kill. He fed on killings just as a vulture would scavenge for carrion.

The early hours of the next day found Grant in the

warm haven that was Hugo Eriksson's home – one of four three-roomed shacks along a railroad siding at Warren Halt. He sat in the parlour, comfortable in an old cushioned wingback chair, close to a fire that Hugo's feisty young wife, Laura, had stoked into roaring life. Soon he was spooning strengthening gruel through his teeth.

Hugo was a small man with a bad leg. He hovered in the background, seemingly happy that his young wife was showing such care for the man he had brought home. Eriksson had worked for the railroad since he had been discharged from the Union army at the end of the Civil War, glad enough, as a permanent cripple, to find employment. Rebel grapeshot had raked him across the hips during the awesome battle of Antioch, rendering his left leg pretty useless, but the Swede did a good job on the footplate of a locomotive and had proved a loyal employee of the Union Pacific Railroad.

And so the weeks slipped by.

It was Christmas Eve and Laura had fixed a branch of cottonwood in the corner of the parlour to represent a tree. She'd decorated it with coloured ribbons and tassels.

'Grant,' she said as he helped her dunk the turkey in a pan of scalding water, 'you can't mourn over that boy Joe Evans for the rest of your life.'

Yesterday her husband had brought the bird home and tomorrow, after he returned from work, they would enjoy a feast.

A moment later as Grant sat at the table, helping

Laura pluck the softened feathers from the carcass, he tried to draw his mind away from deep melancholy. He knew she was right, but much of what he saw seemed to solidify into Joe's youthful features, even the pile of feathers on the table, even the flames that flickered up from the log in the grate. Joe Evans had deserved better than a bullet in the head, and Grant blamed himself for the death of the boy. Even more, he blamed the leader of the vigilantes. Hatred for Seth Fryer burned into him like an infected carbuncle. Once he got his strength back he would make the man pay for what he had done, but now all he could do was shudder as he thought of how the boy's mother and sister must be grieving.

The wind was whistling an unholy tune in the chimney.

'Grant,' Laura said, somehow wrapping her tongue around his name as if it were a cherry. 'How come you quit being a lawman down in Texas?'

'Oh,' he responded, 'things were so law-abiding where I was, that I got plumb bored with the job.' He could have told her much more, about how it hadn't always been that lawful, but with his jaw sewn up, lengthy conversation became a strain.

His gaze settled on Laura's hands – slender, efficient hands that stripped away the feathers far more quickly than his own did. When the bird was naked, she took an axe and cleaved off its head, then its feet. She rolled her gingham sleeves back and reached, two-handed, deep inside the bird. She extracted the membrane, intestines and lungs in a single glistening mass and, with a knife, cut carefully around the excretory vent, freeing the viscera and dropping them into a bowl.

She raised the side of her mouth in a wry smile. 'Womenfolk always get the dirty jobs to do.'

He nodded, knowing that she liked him to watch her. Sometimes she would check to make sure his gaze was on her. Why did she look so beautiful, with her hands messy and the firelight catching the glint in her eyes and hair? He imagined her as some pagan goddess. A flush of envy touched him. How come a wreck of a man like Hugo Eriksson, little more than a dwarf and crippled in the Civil War, had persuaded a female, twenty years his junior, to marry him and spend her days in a run-down railroad shack on a siding at the back of nowhere?

A week ago, he'd watched her gazing wistfully through the window at the neighbour's children as they built a snowman, and he thought maybe some offspring of her own would be good for her.

Grant had spent too many hours alone with this woman while her husband was at work, sensing in her a strange glee, a mischievousness, that troubled him. It would be best for them all, he told himself, when he could get back to work. It had been six weeks since Hugo Eriksson had offered him the hospitality of his humble home.

Laura had fussed over him like an attentive nanny, preparing soft food that would slip between his teeth and give him the sustenance he needed. The ability to communicate his gratitude had been limited. All he could manage were brief words through his clamped jaw, feeling like the ventriloquist he'd once seen at a travelling circus. But gradually he realized that Laura yearned for his thanks in a different way, and the knowledge filled him with guilt. He had abstained from womanly comfort for what seemed an eternity. Now, watching her, he feared that his powers of resistance would crumble and cause him to betray the man who had proved one of the best friends he'd ever had.

She ladled water into a basin and washed the carcass, extracting the last pinfeathers and the odd particle of tooth-chipping bird-shot. 'When it's dry, I'll rub the skin with salt and oil.' Her dark hair had somehow come loose and she looked at him through a wayward lock. 'How come you haven't got a wife?' she asked forthrightly. 'A good-looking fellow like you needs a woman.'

He sighed. She never pulled her punches. 'I had a wonderful wife,' he admitted through clenched teeth. 'Her name was Josephine but...' he shrugged his shoulders, 'she died of diphtheria.'

She frowned and said, 'I'm sure sorry, Grant.'

He drew himself up, anxious to change the subject. 'Laura, I guess my jaw's just about healed. I best go and see the doctor and get my teeth opened up.'

'Hugo told me,' she said, 'the doctor who fixed your jaw has moved to Barclay. Taken over the surgery of the doctor who was killed.'

He nodded, surprised. He didn't fancy a trip to Barclay, not yet, even though Hugo had told him the railroad had confirmed that he was their employee and not an outlaw. 'That'll get Fryer off your back,' Hugo had assured him.

'I could unfix your jaw for you,' Laura said. 'If I can gut a fowl, there's no reason I can't do a small job like that. Maybe you could enjoy some solid turkey-meat tomorrow. Wouldn't do you no harm.'

He swallowed hard. The thought appealed to him. 'Are you sure you could do it?'

She smoothed her hair into place with the back of her hand. Her smile came again, somehow saying things her tongue did not. 'I could do it.'

When the bird was ready for cooking, she slipped it into the big Franklin oven and stoked up the fire, then she disappeared into her bedroom and presently returned with a small pair of scissors. She'd removed her apron.

'Sit in the chair by the fire, Grant, rest your head back.'

He complied, settling into the wing-backed chair, feeling the warmth of the fire, hearing the fury of snow and wind against the outside walls. The turkey was making a crackling sound from the oven.

'Glad we're inside, nice and cosy,' she said. She raised the hem of her gingham dress and slid astride his knees. He noticed how casually the buttons of her square-necked dress were fastened, half-in, half-out, of their holes. In fact the top one came undone as she leaned over him, the sheer weight of her breasts over-whelming its restraining power. 'Open your lips, honey,' she whispered.

Gently, her fingers probed his teeth and he sensed rather than felt the snip of the scissors as she drew out fragments of twine and placed them on a plate at the side. She worked for a long time, pressing ever closer so that he felt every curve and cranny she possessed, the bulge of her pelvis, even the hard knots of her nipples, and he knew she was naked beneath her dress. He was breathing so heavily that she chided him to keep still. ' 'Less you want me to cut your tongue out at the same time!'

'But Laura,' he somehow gasped, 'if Hugo was to come home, catch us like this . . .'

She hushed the words with her fingers, snipping away with the scissors. 'Hugo won't be home till tomorrow,' she whispered.

The scent of her enveloped him. He guessed she had dabbed some lavender behind her ears and maybe elsewhere. And she was behaving with the naïvety of a little girl, as if she was totally unaware that the weight of her body was pinning him to the chair, that the second button of her dress had surrendered under the strain and that the pale fullness of her bosom was scant inches from his face.

'Honey,' she whispered, 'I guess it's all out now.'

He hesitated, then caught her meaning. He flexed his stiff jaw, enjoying a freedom he had not known for six weeks. 'That's real kind of you, Laura,' he murmured, his tongue clumsy after being imprisoned for so long.

He noticed how the naïvety had dissolved from her face, replaced by a belief that she had trapped him, that it was no longer necessary to play games.

'The least you can do is pay me back, honey.' She smiled coyly. 'I'll be real mindful of your recent indisposition.' Suddenly she slipped her hands around his neck, supporting his head, her moist lips coming to his. Pinned beneath her, nigh smothered, he could do nothing but respond, blind to everything apart from the passion of her kiss, the vibrant lust of her body.

Still astride him, she drew back, forced by the need to breathe, her expression triumphant. 'Glory, Grant!' she gasped. 'I've been wanting to do that for weeks.' Her fingers were quivering as she unfastened the remaining buttons of her dress and shrugged it from her shoulders. He gazed up through the valley of her bosom, seeing how her hair had plunged forward again, glimpsing the wicked, dreamy glint in her eyes, the sheer puffy wantonness of the lips he'd fed on. She cupped her hands beneath her breasts, leaned forward again. 'Kiss them, honey,' she gasped. 'For God's sake kiss them or I'll die!'

'But you're a married woman, Laura.' He squirmed, fighting a battle to remain passive. 'No. It's not right.'

'Glory!' She emitted a wildcat snarl. She still straddled him, her dress crumpled around her waist like a discarded chastity belt.

It was at that moment that the door had burst open, the frigidity of wind and snow cutting into the parlour with needle sharpness, the roar of the outside blizzard smashing into their hammering senses, setting the flames in the hearth dancing in alarm.

Groaning with dismay, Grant glanced over Laura's naked shoulder and saw Hugo Eriksson poised in the doorway.

His mouth sagging, the Swede stood as if frozen in time, the snow clinging to his whiskers, his face reddened by exposure to the elements.

'Snow's blocking the line,' he said. 'Trains can't get through. That's why I'm home early.'

ELEVEN

Spring seemed long in coming that year, but when it arrived it made up for lost time. The winter winds shrivelled and died, the snow melted and creeks were running and full of trout. The meadows became covered in lush grass and crocus blooms tainted the air with their sharp and slender perfumes.

After the scene at Eriksson's shack, Grant had not delayed his return to work. He'd felt shocked at the sudden appearance of his friend that night, and even more shocked by the Swede's words.

Eriksson was switched to another line, and Grant did not see him after he walked out that night. All the Texan could do was brood on his shame. At first he buried himself in clerical work at the railroad office in Catto, allowing his jaw to return to normality. And all along, he heard no word of Fryer or the events surrounding him. But he knew that he could not put off inspecting the track to Barclay for ever. It lay like a challenge in his mind. So did the fact that sooner or later he was determined to bring Seth Fryer to account. Hence, one sunny May day, he ran his handcar along the rails overshadowed by Pilgrim's Pinnacle, the hairs on the nape of his neck itching as he wondered if any twisted-minded gunmen lurked in the rocks, gazing at his vulnerable back. He tried to shrug off the thought.

He completed his inspection, finding the track sound, and arrived in Barclay in the early part of the afternoon. He felt obliged to visit Joe's mother and sister, to express his sadness and explain to them what had happened.

After he had parked his handcar in a siding, he entered the town, keeping a wary eye open for anybody who might dislike him. Things were pretty quiet with not many folks on the raised boardwalks, just a few horses hitched outside the saloon. His mind kept tugging at past events. He still felt puzzled that the Reverend Hendrix had accompanied Fryer at the time Joe Evans had been shot. Had he joined Fryer's vigilantes? It seemed most unlikely for a minister of the church to undertake such violent duty. He guessed he would have to visit the reverend and get a few questions answered. But first, something caught his eye – a handbill pinned to a telegraph pole.

ELECT SETH FRYER AS YOUR TOWN SHERIFF

The State Legislature has approved the appointment of a Town Sheriff in Barclay. Election for this post will take place June 1. There is no better man than Seth Fryer to serve the community as he has already proved as Chairman of the Vigilantes.

Grant cursed. A lawman's badge would give Fryer even greater opportunity to satisfy his lust to kill. He wondered if there was anybody standing in opposition for the job. Would anybody dare put their life on the line and stand against such a fearful man?

He found the Evans house and knocked at the door. There was no response, so he knocked again. Still no answer, but from the corner of his eye he fancied he saw a slight movement in the curtain of the upstairs window. He waited a while, then walked on, disappointed. While he would not admit it to himself, the prospect of again seeing Joe's sister, eighteen-year-old Kathryn, had appealed to him.

He reached the church but did not enter. His discussion with the reverend could wait till later. He took the trail, fringed with cottonwoods, out of town, exchanging greetings with odd passers-by. They did not know him any more than he knew them, but folks were friendly enough when the sunshine was warm and the air redolent with spring.

He knew the cemetery lay on the far side of a hillock, shielded from winter winds and storms, and it was to this that he was headed, to pay his respects at the graveside of young Joe Evans.

But very little can happen in a small Western community, even though the sidewalks appear deserted, without word of events getting around. Grant's earlier fears about returning to Barclay had been well founded. He should have stayed away.

The gate through the surrounding fence of the cemetery stood open, as if to say 'all are welcome'. He glanced around the fifty-odd markers; they were mostly planks of weathered wood, some leaning haphazardly amid the sprouting grass, but there were a few more elegant markers of hand-chipped granite rock. The place possessed a deathly silence, like a vacuum of loneliness, more profound than any other place he had known. He concluded that he was the only visitor this afternoon, apart from the butterflies which flitted prettily in the sunshine and the buzzard that cruised disconcertingly on the high thermals above. Despite his sombre mood, Grant couldn't help but smile as he noticed the inscription on one stone. The incumbent had left a message for those still alive:

Remember that as you are,
so once was I,
and as I am you soon will be.
Remember me.

The burial lots were pretty tightly packed, but Grant soon found what he was seeking. The newest of the granite markers was at the far corner, still white and untouched by moss, its inscription freshly chipped:

Here Lies Joe Evans
Beloved Son and Twin Brother
1860–1878
Murdered by a Coward

At the foot of the stone was a vase of fresh violets, no doubt recently placed by a loving hand.

He hunkered down beside the grave, his finger touching the boy's inscribed name, a prayer coming to his lips, his mind once again focused on memories of

Joe's courage and unfulfilled ambitions to become a doctor. What a waste of a life!

The wrongness of it surged through him like a dark wave, and he wanted to reach into the grave, drag Joe out and restore him to life.

Like an unobserved shadow, the Reverend Hendrix had followed Grant, moving stealthily through the cotton-woods, slipping into the cemetery while the railroad man's back was turned.

Hendrix worked his way closer, eventually crouching behind one of the taller stones, his hand caressing the butt of the double-action pistol nestling in his coat pocket. He could feel his excitement rising, breaking a sweat on his face. Yet still his brain focused with catlike clarity. One shot would be all that was necessary, one shot in the head, same as the boy. At this range he couldn't miss, and later he would report that he had found the body in the cemetery, gunned down by an unknown assailant.

Nobody would doubt the word of a reverend.

He took a deep breath, was about to slip the gun from its concealment, when a voice sounded behind him, causing him to straighten up in alarm.

'Good day, Reverend. Thought I'd come up and pay respects to my predecessor, James Brininstool. Could you point out his grave?'

Hendrix had spun round, desperately striving to assume the persona of a humble minister of the Lord, rather than the ruthless killer that he truly was. His gaze rested on Barclay's newest resident, the corpulent Dr Nathan Carter.

The words Hendrix spoke cloaked the fury that simmered behind his false smile. 'You'll find his resting place at the far corner, next to the grave of young Joe Evans. Over where that fellow's standing.'

Grant, hearing voices, had straightened up, unaware of how, yet again, death had reached out to rest its finger on him. He turned to see Dr Carter approaching, while, behind, he glimpsed the reverend, and his pulse quickened.

The medical man expressed his greeting, then gave him a further long glance as recognition dawned. 'Say, didn't I fix that jaw of yours a few weeks back? Weren't you coming for me to remove the fixings?'

Grant nodded. If only he'd heeded the doctor's advice, he might have avoided Laura's catastrophic advances. 'A lady did the work,' he explained. 'Saved you the trouble.'

Carter grunted disapprovingly. 'Better let me take a look at it, young man. Best make certain that fracture has knitted properly. Open up your mouth.'

Feeling like a naughty child, Grant did as he was told, allowing the doctor to peer into his mouth and finger his jaw.

'Seems to have mended OK,' Carter said. 'You're lucky, but you shouldn't let females carry out medical work. No telling what damage they can cause.'

Again Grant nodded, at the same time noting that the reverend had disappeared, fading like a spectre returning to another world.

Meanwhile the doctor had turned his attention to the adjacent grave of James Brininstool, whose practice in Barclay he now ran and whose patients he had inherited, together with the annual fees that many paid to maintain their health. He remarked how untimely the man's death had been and Grant felt sure that he had no idea how closely he had been associated with that demise. He had no intention of enlightening his companion.

Five minutes later the two of them left the cemetery and walked down towards the town. Grant noticed another handbill nailed to a tree: ELECT SETH FRYER AS YOUR SHERIFF . . .

Seeing his interest, Carter said, 'I guess Fryer won't have much opposition. Everybody's scared stiff of him, wouldn't dare cross him. I'd have the fellow kicked out of town tomorrow if I had my way.'

Grant nodded, but his thoughts were running fast. 'I know somebody who might stand against him.'

Carter shot him a puzzled glance. 'It would have to be somebody who's had experience maintaining the law. Somebody who could outsmart a fellow like Fryer.'

'I know somebody who'd fit the bill,' Grant said.

'Who?'

'Me,' Grant murmured.

The doctor chewed that over. He glanced at a felled tree-trunk at the side of the trail. 'Let's sit a while,' he said. 'We could maybe talk things through.'

Grant nodded, knowing that he was half-way to committing himself to something that could change his life. None the less, an hour later he returned to town, went to the newspaper office and ordered a score of posters to be printed and pinned up. *Bring Law and Order to Barclay. Grant Mayo for Sheriff. Meeting 7 p.m. next Tuesday outside the Doctor's Surgery.*

Meanwhile, Dr Carter had promised to have Grant's name legally registered with the mayor as a candidate for the post of sheriff.

TWELVE

Seth Fryer had set out determined to find the railroad man who had caused him nothing but trouble since the abortive lynching. The desire to gain vengeance ran through him like a prairie wind. Stumpy Simmons had told him he'd seen Grant walk down the street after he had knocked, in vain, at the door of the Evans household. Fryer tried to calm his anger. He walked the entire lengths of Barclay's main street and side alleys, enquiring in most of the stores after the man he sought, trying to sound casual – but nobody admitted to having seen Grant. The town was small enough and it took him no more than an hour to determine that his quarry was not around, then he thought about the cemetery. Maybe Grant had gone up there, maybe to visit the grave of Joe Evans. He cursed to himself, reckoning he'd best walk out there and find out. But first, he decided to ask at the railroad station.

The clerk in the ticket-office pointed to the siding where Grant's handcar was parked. 'If you wait there, he's sure to come back,' he explained. 'Ain't in no more trouble, is he?'

Fryer didn't respond. He took up position between

some sheds at the side of the track, where he was partially hidden. He loosened his gun in its holster, hunkered down in some shade, his cumbersome body sweating with impatience.

Anne Evans went white as she opened the front door of her house and realized that it had been Grant who had knocked.

'I wanted to say how sorry I am about Joe,' he said, knowing how inadequate his words were.

She hesitated, opened her mouth to speak, but said nothing.

'May I come in, Mrs Evans?' he enquired, never feeling too happy about having his back turned to the street.

Again she hesitated, then gave her head a stiff nod. 'Yes . . . yes, of course.' She stood back. He removed his cap and entered the small parlour, memories of his last visit flooding back to him. On the dresser he noticed a tintype photograph of Joe Evans, smiling with his hair combed neatly. Beside the picture was a portrait of a handsome bearded man, no doubt his deceased father. Grant felt a wave of compassion for this decimated family.

'Sit down,' Anne Evans said. 'I'll fetch you a drink.'

He nodded his thanks and lowered himself on to a chair. She went into a back room and he heard a drawer slide open, then close. He wondered if Kathryn was home, but he concluded not. The house seemed so quiet. The grandfather clock, standing in the corner of the parlour, ticked with solemn dignity.

He heard the woman's footstep, turned and gasped.

He was gazing into the muzzle of a six-shooter. The revolver was held two-handed, aimed at his chest.

'Why. . . ?' His mouth sagged.

'You'll get no welcome here, Grant,' she said, malevolence radiating from her green eyes. 'Raise your hands before I pull the trigger. You deserve to be gunned down in the same way as you shot my Joe!'

Still sitting, Grant raised his hands. 'But, Mrs Evans, I never—'

'Don't tell lies,' she cried. 'Seth Fryer told me what happened that day in Catto.'

He took a deep breath, trying to calm himself. He could see how white her knuckles were as she gripped the gun, how distraught her emotions were.

'What did he tell you?' he asked.

'As if you didn't know!' she said.

He wondered if the poor woman had lost her wits. 'What did he tell you?' he repeated.

'He told us how you shot poor Joe, how you turned on him and shot him in the . . . head.' She faltered, choking on her grief.

'I did no such thing,' he cried out indignantly. 'How could I? I didn't have a gun, not that I would've shot Joe. He'd saved my life. He was a wonderful friend to me, Mrs Evans. I owed him nothing but gratitude, and you too, for sheltering me that night. He was a fine boy and never deserved to be murdered like that.'

'You're telling me lies, Grant,' she accused him, the gun still pointed at him.

'I'm telling you the truth,' he said. 'Seth Fryer and the reverend were following us. Fryer fired the shot that killed Joe. I swear. If you doubt me, ask the Reverend Hendrix. He saw everything.'

He saw doubt cloud her strained face, saw the first wavering of the gun, but still she wasn't fully convinced. 'Would you swear before God that it was Seth Fryer who shot Joe? Will you swear it on a Holy Bible?'

He met her eyes, saw the intensity of them. 'Yes, ma'am, I surely would.'

Only then was the gun lowered.

'Stay exactly where you are,' she said and stepped out of the room. When she returned, she was holding a Bible. 'Place your hand on it, Grant. God's wrath will be on you if you lie.'

Grant repeated his story, his hand resting on the book.

As he finished, he said, 'And if that's not good enough, we'll go up to the church and, like I said, you can ask the reverend.'

She gave him a long stare. He felt as if she was shining a lantern into his very soul.

'I don't think that will be necessary.' She sat down. All the strength seemed to flow out of her, she started to tremble, and he realized how grief had weakened her. Seeing him, after all she had believed over the past weeks, must have given her a terrible shock.

'Seth Fryer's an evil man,' Grant explained. 'He was too much of a coward to tell you the truth. The only consolation is that Joe died a quick death. He didn't suffer for a moment, Mrs Evans.'

'But why did he shoot Joe?'

'He believed that he had murdered Doctor Brininstool, that's why. He shot him down without giving a chance to explain matters. In his mind, he has a cast-iron reason for killing Joe, and nobody will stand up to him.'

She sighed and sat with her face buried in her hands for a moment. At last she lifted her eyes to his. He sat with her for maybe an hour, telling her all that had happened to him, even how Doctor Brininstool had been shot, and she listened attentively, her face reflecting the misery of her feelings.

Suddenly the chime of the clock reminded Grant of the time. He had to get back to his handcar and return to Catto before nightfall. He felt satisfied that he had convinced Anne Evans of his innocence, but he sensed that while Seth Fryer ruled the roost in this town, there would be no true justice.

From his hiding-place, with the evening shadows lengthening, Seth Fryer snapped to alertness. His attention focused on Grant as he came up the street. He growled with jealousy. Anne Evans was walking alongside the railroad man, talking to him as if he was an old friend.

Fryer drew his gun, the prospect of killing the man he hated bringing an exhilaration throbbing through his veins, but suddenly doubts assailed him. The clerk in the railroad office had been well aware of Fryer's presence, even caught his eye and nodded acknowledgement as he left his ticket-window to stretch his legs. Similarly, there were a half-dozen or so folk standing on the platform, awaiting a train. The crack of a gun, the killing of Grant, would draw immediate attention. Fryer realized that he would not be able to escape from his present position unseen. If folks realized that he had gunned down a seemingly unarmed man, it would not help with his ambitions to be elected as town sheriff. Furthermore, such an act would alienate Anne Evans from him for ever.

He slid his gun back into its holster. By the look on her face, Anne Evans no longer hated Grant. Fryer wondered how Grant had convinced her he was not guilty of her son's murder, and even worse, had he told her the true facts surrounding the boy's death? The thought brought a sour taste to Fryer's mouth. He swore he'd get even with Grant, but now was not the moment, so he retreated unseen from his position near the railroad station and ten minutes later he was back at his cabin, determined to think up a new means of disposing of Grant. One thing was certain. He could not abide life, while he was obliged to share it with the damned railroad man. There was not room for both of them in this world.

Next morning his hatred was fanned to white heat. One of his vigilantes dropped into his cabin with a poster he'd torn down from a telegraph pole: *Grant Mayo for Sheriff* . . . Fryer almost burst a blood vessel.

THIRTEEN

Strangely, it was not the prospect of challenging Seth Fryer for the post of own sheriff that troubled Grant in his dreams that night, but visions of Laura Eriksson. When he awoke, sweating with thoughts of passion, it took him some minutes to convince himself that she was not in the bed with him, her warm, receptive body pressed against him, her breath burning his cheek as she whispered his name over and over. It was his shout that lifted him from his restless slumber. *Laura, no!*

Now he lay uncovered, his crumpled blanket tossed aside, fearful that his cry might have awakened old Mrs Tolly, his landlady. But he heard no stirring from her room along the landing. The thin light of pre-dawn was seeping through his window, the first chirps of early birds were heralding the day. He rose from his bed, went to his washstand, dipped his hands into the jug and splashed cold water on to his sweating face. God! Thoughts of Laura had stirred him and guilt swelled in him, seeming more threatening, more destructive than anything else he'd suffered.

He returned to his bed, sat down upon it. If he closed his eyes, he was confronted by a vision of Hugo

Eriksson's sudden appearance that night, cloaked with snow, his eyes glinting at the sight of his wife half-naked with a man whom he had saved from terrible danger. What a way to repay his kindness!

Grant had scrambled up, thrusting Laura unceremoniously aside, finding there was nothing he could say to soften the harshness of that moment, the overwhelming sensation of betrayal.

To his astonishment, Laura had smoothed her dress into place, walked to her husband, slipped her arms around his neck and hugged herself to him, her weeping blending with the howl of the outside wind.

Grant's fears had been ill directed. Circumstances were far more complex than anything he'd suspected. He could scarcely believe what he had heard that night – the stunning words that had come from Eriksson's lips.

One thing was certain. He could linger with the Erikssons no longer. Fully fit or not, he must return to work.

Following his visit to Barclay, his homage at the grave of Joe Evans, his brush with death, albeit unbeknown to himself, and his long talk with Anne Evans, Grant concentrated each day on his work. He checked the rails west of Catto, finding no faults apart from those caused by the routine passage of trains. His strength had returned and now he prepared himself for a change of employment, a return to his old work of keeping the law. But first, he knew, he had to carry out considerable groundwork. He had to capture the support of the Barclay townsfolk. Accordingly, he spent his evenings preparing notes for the speech he intended to make. It would be a means of introducing himself, of convincing people that he was a man who could free the town of injustice, mysterious and violent deaths, of fear.

The Tuesday of the meeting he had called came with surprising speed, and by seven o'clock he was outside Dr Carter's surgery, standing on the raised sidewalk, surrounded by bright-yellow posters appealing for votes. Standing alongside him were the doctor and Anne Evans. Also present was Kathryn Evans, easily convinced by her mother how foolish they had been to believe Seth Fryer's monstrous lies. Kathryn had said she'd never believed Grant was guilty.

But fate was not kind on this occasion. A steady rain had begun to fall and turnout was poor – no more than a dozen, including the mayor, Aaron Creswell, wearing his gold chain. He was also the local banker, a big, blue-eyed man with an often jovial manner. Grant had wondered if Fryer himself might appear and spark some sort of debate, but there was no sign of him. Maybe he considered it beneath his dignity and that such opposition was not worth considering.

It seemed that people were either totally uninterested, or too afraid of Fryer and his vigilantes, to support any upstart opposition. Apparently, Fryer had held a meeting on the previous day and this had been well attended.

Cresswell introduced Grant, speaking with a flair he obviously enjoyed. He'd done the same for Seth Fryer the day before, though with less enthusiasm.

When Grant stepped forward, he shielded his disappointment at the meagreness of the attendance. He spoke passionately about decent law and order, about his previous experience as a deputy in Texas, about every man's right to a fair trial before he faced punishment. He promised that if elected he would serve the town of Barclay with honesty and utmost endeavour, ensuring that its streets were safe to walk, that unruly behaviour would not be tolerated. He emphasized that fear could have no place when fair law and order and true justice held sway.

He made no mention of Fryer by name, but his implications left no doubt in the hearts of those who listened that evening.

He finished to a ripple of applause. He asked for questions. None came, individuals appearing anxious to escape the rain, but the mayor shook his hand, expressing admiration for his courage in standing against the formidable opposition.

The first day of June, Election Day, swept up on the town of Barclay with amazing swiftness, but there seemed little excitement, for the outcome seemed a foregone conclusion. Perhaps the most noteworthy aspect of the election was the fact that Wyoming had enacted women's suffrage, being one of the first territories to acknowledge that females had as much right to express an opinion with regard to the running of the country as did men. The more grudging of males, however, said that such suffrage had been necessary in order to attract more women into this part of the West.

The day dawned bright and sunny. Seth Fryer had had three great banners strung across the main street, extolling his claim for the post of town sheriff. Grant couldn't afford any greater publicity for his candidacy than a few brightly coloured posters. But he guessed word of him had spread through the town, not necessarily for his likely ability to win the election, but for his sheer audacity in standing against Fryer.

The mayor had set up two tables as desks outside the saloon. Electors were instructed to form lines, one for each candidate. The mayor and his clerk supervised the polling and each voter had his or her hand stamped with blue dye to prevent their voting again. Seth Fryer mingled amongst the townsfolk, looming over them, uncharacteristically smiling and shaking hands and acting as if he was everybody's friend. Everybody's friend, that was, apart from Grant, to whom he didn't even extend a glance. Folks had never seen Seth Fryer so affable. Grant guessed he might just have well not have been standing as far as Fryer was concerned, and this seemed to be confirmed as a long line of voters stood at the vigilante's table, while but a handful, mostly ladies, recorded their votes in Grant's favour. Within an hour, there was no doubt about the result and Grant accepted defeat, shaking the mayor's hand and thanking him for the way he'd organized the election. He then walked across to where Fryer stood in the shade of a stoop and acknowledged his victory. Fryer turned his back and walked away.

Over the following weeks, Fryer sold his cabin, moved in above the newly erected sheriff's office and concentrated full time on what he perceived other people would consider to be his lawful duties. In truth he was an individual of evil desires and lusts, and in addition, he was a lonely, unloved man.

Since his election, he had taken to patrolling the town, his lawman's badge pinned to his shirt, his mere approach causing townsfolk to whisper his name in warning and move aside. Knowledge of the ruthless manner in which he would treat the sins of others was common knowledge.

One sultry afternoon, he wandered up to the nearby crest and gazed down on what he considered to be his dominion, the town of Barclay, with its church, bank and saloon. He frowned. There had been no suggestion of crime since he had taken office and this annoyed him, because he longed to conduct a trial and the resultant hanging. He was glad he had put Grant in his place, although the fact that he had not been able to dispose of him irked him.

His gaze swung across to the deserted, white-fenced cemetery on the adjacent hillside and he thought of Joe Evans. He wasn't sure if the boy's mother now associated him with the death. The fact that her attitude towards him continued to be cold might have been due to other reasons, reasons that he was determined to rectify. He was town sheriff now and she should realize that she owed him respect.

He walked over the hillside, reached the cemetery and entered by the gate. He towered over the grave of Joe Evans, removing his hat as a sign of apparent respect for the benefit of anybody who might be watching.

Anne Evans had no reason to hate him, he told himself. He had assured her he was not to blame for the death of her son, but he couldn't tell what Grant had told her. The thought of Grant angered him and he swore under his breath, then censured himself for such thoughts here at the graveside. He made a conscious effort to soften his thoughts. Anne Evans would never favour him unless he showed her that he had a tender side to his nature. He sighed, guessing he must make an effort to court the woman. Perhaps he would start this very evening and take her some flowers. The fresh daffodils on the boy's grave caught his fancy and he glanced around to make sure he was unobserved before stooping down. His fingers had touched the flowers before he recalled that Anne had probably placed them on the grave herself. He would have to find some other means of softening her attitude. But one thing was certain: one way or other, he intended to have her.

Fryer returned to his room above the sheriff's office, his mind made up. He would not be fobbed off any more. He prepared himself carefully, putting on a clean shirt, and combing his hair and moustache. Looking in the mirror, he told himself his very ugliness made him distinctive. What woman, in her right mind, would reject him?

He was leaving his room when he swung back, picked up the sheriff's badge from the washstand. He pinned it to his coat, grunting with pride. He had almost forgotten it, but this symbol of power was important, indicating that right was on his side.

Anne Evans paused in her fruit-peeling as she heard the knock at the front door. She was still garbed in black, having no desire to cease mourning for her son. She peered between the curtains of her window and sighed as she recognized her visitor. She hesitated, then convinced herself that she must face this man. She could not shy away from him and his advances for ever. She opened her door, felt herself enveloped by the aura of his presence.

His voice came with unusual humility. 'Anne, my dear, can I come in? I need to talk with you.'

She hesitated. He removed his hat and ducked through the doorway, brushing past her before she could respond. She clenched her hands into fists, hating him for his roughness. The animal stench of his body wafted to her.

'I have urgent matters to talk of, Anne.' He glanced around and asked, 'Where's Kathryn?'

'She's gone to visit her aunt in Miles City,' Anne Evans said, and immediately regretted that she'd revealed she was at home alone.

Fryer nodded, then said, 'I have something important to ask.'

Even in her prim black, the physical nearness of her excited him. For years he had watched her, allowing his imagination and frustrations to run wild. How he longed to peel the dress away from her breasts, to run his hands over her womanliness, to possess her body in all its intimacy.

'I've been elected sheriff fair and square,' he said. 'It's a respected position for a man, but I need a wife, Anne, somebody to share my position in town society. I . . .'

He paused. He had never been good at talking to the opposite sex, and he squirmed behind this façade of humility. He wished he had brought her some flowers.

He gazed at her face, seeing no softening in her features, no understanding, no compassion, just the rise and fall of her bodice with each deep gasp of breath. He steeled himself. 'Anne, will you be my wife?'

Sudden defiance flared in her eyes. 'Not in a million years, Seth Fryer!'

An animal-like growl came from his throat. He raised his great paw to her arm, gripped it, hanging on despite her attempts to shrug him off.

'I'm not used to being treated like scum,' he shouted, the mock sweetness gone from him, 'not by man nor woman.'

She winced at his tightening grip. 'Then get out,' she said, 'because that's the only way you'll be treated here!'

At last she twisted free of his grip, rubbing her arm where he'd held her.

'I'm sorry,' he said, but there was an angry edge to his voice. He made a conscious effort to control himself. 'You don't have to decide this moment. I can come back this evening and we can talk things over. Make our plans for the future, eh?'

'I've already made my decision,' she said coolly. 'I don't love you, never have done, despite what happened. Leave me alone. I want no part of you!'

She watched incredulity come to his deep-set eyes, watched it replaced by a feral lust that she had never seen before. Spittle glistened on his drawn-back lips and the veins in his forehead were pulsing.

He lunged at her, his hands tearing at the bodice of her black dress, like a starved man grabbing at food. Her cries intensified his determination. He had sworn he would have her. Whether she wanted him or not didn't matter!

She fought him like a cat, enflaming his fury beyond all reasonable bounds. He ripped the dress from her body. The sharpness of the pain her blows inflicted increased the fury and lust within him, and he over-powered her like an unstoppable storm-torrent, his hands shifting from the pale softness of her breasts to her throat. As she fell back on to the parlour boards, his snarls were of sheer carnality and his immense weight crushed her. Passion pounded in his head, his huge hands gripped her throat and his thumbs choked out her shrieking. He lost count of time, ecstasy forcing the breath from his lungs in shuddering gasps. At last he sagged down, spent, oblivious to the fact that her strug-gling had ceased, that her body no longer resisted him in any way.

At last he drew back, shifted clear of her, his chest heaving. Slowly reality dawned on him.

Anne Evans was dead and he had killed her. For a long moment he revelled in the ecstasy that this knowledge brought him. But gradually he felt his sweat turn cold and other thoughts came into his head. Hanging or shooting down some riffraff of a man, some criminal, was one thing, something that the community would approve of. But killing Anne Evans was a different matter and would not be accepted.

He sobbed then, sobbed like a baby.

He staggered to his feet, seeing how the sky had darkened outside. His big hands were shaking as he drew over the curtains for fear that somebody might peer in. Nobody must associate him with what had happened here.

He moved into the bedroom, gathered up a blanket from the bed. He returned to the parlour, for a moment not wishing to gaze upon the crumpled, half-naked body of the woman. In fact he averted his eyes as his hands went to work, pulling the remnants of her dress, underclothing and blanket over the body. He glanced around. He must make sure there was no evidence of his presence. He scurried about, straightening the furniture and tidying. When he was finished, he left by the back door, carrying the blanket-shrouded corpse, glad enough that the shadows in the back alley concealed him. He reached the rear part of the sheriff's office, found a spade and within minutes had saddled his horse and mounted up, resting his burden in front of him.

He left town, avoiding the main street, keeping to the shadowy scrubland and presently followed the rail-line along, glad that, so far as he could tell, he had not been seen. All was not yet lost.

FOURTEEN

Frank Clayton rode past Pilgrim's Pinnacle remembering the chaos of his last venture into this neck of the woods. He grimaced as he recalled how the gang had waited on that freezing night for the cash-bearing train to appear and, when it did not, how the vigilantes had surprised them. It had been a miracle that all the gang had escaped and scattered to their hideaways, alive but empty-handed. Now it was time to rectify that situation and lay plans for the next venture. That was why he was on his way to see Hendrix, or the Reverend Benjamin Hendrix as he preferred to be known.

This was not the first visit Clayton had made. On the first occasion, being wounded, he had been glad of Hendrix's hospitality, and found surprisingly fertile ground in the mind of the minister as he had spoken of crime. Since then, he had posed as a clerical friend of Hendrix, his visits always preceding some crime, but of course nobody gave a thought to the fact that the saintly pair were in any way responsible.

Clayton had paused in a copse of spruce, tethered his mount and removed his clerical suit and hat from his saddlebag. He shed his trail-soiled clothes and put on his disguise, in good spirits and feeling sure, as he contemplated the next heist the gang would contrive, that better luck would prevail than had at the last attempt. For a moment he stood in the moonlight, buttoning his coat and straightening his hat and enjoying the peacefulness of the forest. He was about to mount up for the final leg of his journey to Barclay, when a strange sound caught his ear – a clink of metal biting into the gritty soil.

He was tempted to ride on, to leave whatever strange events were taking place in this lonely place well alone. Maybe it was a ghost or some such thing. But as the sound persisted, his curiosity got the better of him, and, placing his feet carefully, he crept towards the source of the sound.

Three minutes later, he paused in the shadows at the fringe of a small clearing in the trees and before him was a sight that made him inwardly gasp. A figure was visible, an immense and cumbersome black figure bathed in ghostly moonlight. The rasp of his heavy breathing carried clearly to the hidden Clayton, who now witnessed how the man was spading something into the earth, something that appeared to be swathed in a blanket, and then shovelling earth on top. When this was done, the giant spent a good ten minutes flattening the ground with his immense weight, doing his obvious and furtive best to conceal the spot of the burying.

Clayton had no desire to linger. The size of the

man he watched, the aura of sinister threat that emanated from him, had him retreating fast. Still unobserved, and praying that his boots would avoid any brittle twigs, he backtracked to his horse, mounted up and spurred the beast onward towards Barclay. As he rode he was troubled not only by the mystery of what he had seen, but also by a glimmer of recognition that plagued him. There was something about the stance of that immense figure that was familiar. It was almost as if the giant represented something from a nightmare. Clayton cursed himself for stupidity and rode on. He figured that whatever was going on was no business of his and was probably well left alone.

It was into the small hours when he reached Barclay. Main Street was silent and deserted, not even a drunk to be seen sleeping it off on the sidewalk. He spared the bank a sideways glance as he passed, and a few minutes later he reached the church and drew rein. Soon, he had roused the Reverend Hendrix from his bed, set his horse to graze in the moonlit meadow. By the time he had taken to his blanket behind the altar, Hendrix had implanted a seed in his mind – a seed that immediately started to grow. Soon the seed would develop to fruition as the two men laid plans for their next project, that of robbing Aaron Creswell's bank in Barclay itself. Admittedly, it was on Hendrix's doorstep, but the idea appealed to him.

So intrigued was Clayton at the prospect, that it was not until the following afternoon that he recalled what he had seen on the previous night and related events to

Hendrix. The reverend shook his head, puzzled. As far as he knew, there was only one man who fitted the description of the individual Clayton had seen, and he couldn't have imagined what Seth Fryer would have been up to at that time of night.

Hendrix decided that he would get Clayton to take him to the spot and check out matters himself. He might discover something that could be turned towards achieving his own ends.

Later that morning, Kathryn Evans stepped down from the stagecoach that had brought her from Miles City. She had spent a week with her aunt. She smoothed the creases from her dress and collected her valise, then she walked the short distance along the street to her home, nodding a smiling greeting to various acquaintances. She was looking forward to seeing her mother again, having only reluctantly left her, for Anne still grieved at the loss of her son. Typical of her kind nature, she had insisted that her daughter get away for a brief holiday, saying that it would do her good.

Now Kathryn opened the door of the house and stepped inside. She was immediately struck by the silence of the place. Even the grandfather clock had stopped, unwound. There was something unusual about the position of the furniture in the room – the wing-backed chair at a far greater angle to the stove than was normal, the ornaments on the dresser in a completely different order from usual. As Kathryn stepped forward, she noticed a small vase, broken with its pieces scattered half-hidden beneath the dresser –

and amid the pieces, her sharp eyes spotted a button. She picked it up.

The button was strange to her. It still had thread attached to it as if it had been torn off forcibly. She slipped it into her pocket.

With concern mounting, Kathryn searched the remaining rooms, all of which seemed in order, apart from the fact that a blanket was missing. But her mother was nowhere around, and Kathryn felt sure she would not have gone out, knowing that her daughter was arriving back home that morning.

Shortly, she had enquired at their neighbours', at the nearby stores and stables, and learned nothing of her mother's whereabouts. Some folks thought she had gone to Miles City with Kathryn, for she had not been seen for some days.

Highly distressed, Kathryn felt she must inform the town sheriff of her mother's disappearance and she hurried to Seth Fryer's office.

Fryer peered over the curtain of his sheriff's office, seeing the girl rushing along the sidewalk. He had heard that she had returned from her absence and knew that it was inevitable she would approach him, seeking his help to discover the whereabouts of her mother. He smiled grimly, telling himself that he'd been too soft of late. He told himself if Kathryn proved too troublesome, he would find a way of dealing with her. But initially he would play her along, even offer her fatherly comfort. In fact perhaps she would be more appreciative of him than her mother had been. He composed himself, sitting behind his desk, as the outer door rattled open and the flushed-faced girl entered. Even in her harassed state, it occurred to him how like Anne Evans her daughter was – the same prettiness, the same womanliness.

'My dear, what is it?' he said in his most comforting voice. 'Sit down and tell me what brings you.'

Kathryn gave her head a rapid shake. 'My mother,' she gasped. 'She's disappeared. Nobody's seen her for days.'

'Disappeared!' Fryer gave his head a disbelieving shake. 'Surely not. I thought she'd gone to Miles City with you.'

'No, she stayed at home and now she's nowhere to be found. I'm so worried. I don't know . . .'

'Calm down, my dear. I'm sure there'll be some reasonable explanation.' Fryer stood up, stepped around his desk and rested his big hand upon her shoulder in his idea of a soothing gesture.

It was at that moment that her glance paused upon the freshly sewn button on his coat. She noticed it because the thread was of a different colour from the others, but immediately her mind moved on to other things.

'I'll ask around,' he said. 'I'm sure somebody will have seen her. Maybe she left a message. Yes, I'll set investigations in progress straight away. Best thing I can do is start looking at your home. I'll come round now and see if I can find any clue.' He reached for his hat and put it on, assuming a businesslike manner.

As the girl gave a reluctant nod, he was glad he would have the opportunity to return to the Evans house, just to make sure he had left no tell-tale sign of what he'd done. He was conscious of the missing button. He had noticed it was gone from his coat when he got back from burying the woman, and wondered if she might have pulled it off during the struggle. On the other hand, he might have lost it previously for it had been loose for some time. At least now he would have the opportunity to look around and check that it wasn't on the parlour floor.

He sensed that Kathryn resented the supportive hold he took on her arm as they walked to the house, but he insisted. She had no cause to resent him, at least none that she knew of. Had she in any way suspected the truth, she would not have come running to him for help.

Once at the house, he asked for a coffee and, as she set about preparing it, he carried out a tour of the house, saying that he was looking for some note or message that might have slipped into some obscure place. He also checked the parlour floor, satisfying himself that no discarded button was evident. It never occurred to him that the button in question was already residing in the pocket of Kathryn's dress.

As she brought him coffee, the strain etched into her young face, Fryer was shaking his head. 'Can't find anything here, my dear. I'll have to widen my searching. I'll do everything I can. You just wait at home here until I have some news. Try not to worry overmuch. I'm sure there's an explanation. Anne isn't the sort of woman to go gallivanting off without telling anybody.'

By the time he left, he had half-convinced her that he would soon have her mother safely back, but as she closed the door after his departure, her hand slipped into her pocket and touched the button and suspicion swept over her.

The two clergymen, one genuine though having two sides to his character, the other bogus, rode out of town that evening. Two hours later Clayton located the spot from which he had witnessed the strange events of the previous night. So well had Fryer covered his tracks that it took Clayton some time to find the exact place of the burying. However, eventually he pointed to where the soil showed a faint disturbance.

Hendrix had brought a spade, normally used for digging graves. Now he put it to a different type of use – excavating.

He was surprised by what he eventually unearthed, cutting open the blanket to reveal the remains of a female body, the soiled tatters of her black dress still clinging to her pale flesh. Further investigation left no doubt in Hendrix's mind as to the identity of the poor woman.

'What are we going to do?' Clayton enquired.

Hendrix stood for a moment, stroking his jaw as he considered matters. Eventually he said, 'We'll fill in the grave and watch what happens in town. Could be this will prove useful to us.'

'How?' Clayton asked.

Hendrix assumed a conspiratorial expression. 'With Fryer in jail, it'll make robbing the bank much easier.'

Clayton nodded and smiled.

After the soil had been replaced and evidence of their presence had been erased, the two men mounted their horses and returned to town. At the church, Hendrix set about rewriting the sermon he would give on the next Sabbath.

FIFTEEN

News of Anne Evans's disappearance now spread through Barclay like raging flame through a tinder-dry forest. Everybody was talking about it when Grant was next in town and, hardly able to believe what he was hearing, he decided the least he could do was call on Kathryn Evans and offer her his support. He reached the house in early afternoon and his knock, after a long pause, brought the girl to the door. All the freshness of her face had gone and there was blackness beneath her eyes. Only her teeth showed white against the shadows of her face. She moved almost as if she was in a trance.

'I heard,' he said. 'I'm very sad for you, Kathryn. I wish I could help.'

She nodded and said, 'Come in, Grant.'

Once inside, with the door closed, she said, 'Until Ma comes back, Beth Cromwell's staying with me. But she's out shopping right now.'

He nodded. She was gazing at him and he could see how worry had taken its toll in her. She seemed about to break into tears, but she stepped forward and he was astounded to find her arms about him, feeling the

111

shuddering sobs in her body as she hugged him.

'Grant,' she sobbed, 'I'm so worried. I don't know what to do. You're the only person I feel I can trust. Please help me to find out what happened to her.'

A warmth flooded through him. He held her, smoothing her back, touching her hair, whispering consoling words and wishing he could contrive a miracle to rescue her from her despair. He remembered how kind Anne, Kathryn and Joe had been to him after he had been 'lynched'. But it seemed his advent into their lives had brought only misery. Now, it appeared, there was only one of the Evans left.

Presently, when she had dried her eyes and regained some composure, they sat at the parlour table, and she told him how she had returned to the empty house, how she had turned to Seth Fryer for help.

'And has he found any clues about her whereabouts?' Grant asked.

She shook her head. 'I'm so worried, worried about him.'

'Fryer . . . why?' He had no liking for the awesome man himself, but he had hoped that he might have been of some help now that he was sheriff.

'I found this on the parlour floor when I got home,' she said, and she held the button in her palm for him to see.

He examined it. 'Looks as though it's from a man's coat.'

She nodded. 'And I noticed that Fryer had recently replaced a button on his coat. It was stitched with a different thread from the others.'

He shook his head in puzzlement, then the implica-

112

tion dawned on him. 'You mean . . . he must've been in this room!'

'Yes, I think he knows what happened to my mother and he's not letting on.'

'Heavens above!' Grant gasped. He pondered for a moment, the grim possibility firming up in his mind. 'One thing's certain, Kathryn. You need help mighty bad.'

His words brought fresh tears from the girl, and she came to his arms again. He felt strangely humble that she trusted him so much. She was too young, too vulnerable, to face up to the harshness of life alone. Her being robbed of her brother and now, possibly, her mother, victims of the same man, was something that could not go unpunished. He was determined not to betray her trust.

At that moment, they heard the tolling of the church bell calling the faithful to service.

'Put your bonnet on, Kathryn,' he murmured. 'Church will do you good, and we need to do some hard praying.'

'Oh God,' she whispered fervently, 'it's good to have a man telling me what to do. I need your strength, Grant.'

He gazed into her eyes, seeing weariness and desperation. She looked in a mirror and sighed, 'Not a pretty sight.' She tidied her hair, brushing back wayward strands with trembling fingers, then fetched her bonnet and put it on. To him, even in her distress, she seemed pretty, and he was proud to walk up the street with her on his arm.

The church was full that evening. News of Anne

113

Evans's disappearance had thrown a sinister shadow over the community, and folks were turning to the Lord for comfort. As was customary, the town sheriff was in attendance, taking his place on the back pew. Mayor Aaron Creswell, Dr Carter and their families also came to worship.

The Reverend Hendrix introduced Frank Clayton, who stood at his side, to the congregation as the Reverend Robert Cable who was on a pastoral visit to Barclay. Today, Hendrix conducted the service with an air of great solemnity, taking the lead in hymns and prayers of a calibre appropriate to the sombre mood of the worshippers. It was only as he stepped into his pulpit and prepared to give his sermon, that onlookers noticed an unusual tenseness in him. His eyes showed a wideness, an excitement that seemed totally out of character.

'Brothers and sisters,' he began, 'I have some sad news for you. Remember Revelation Chapter twelve, verses nine and ten. Here, we read how a snake was thrown out of heaven, how it landed on earth, fooled everybody and became known as Satan. Now I must tell you that this snake, the evil Satan, is amongst us in our small community of Barclay, poisoning us all and creating evil and sin beyond anything we have ever know.'

A ripple of fear went through the congregation as everybody waited in apprehension for their minister's next words. At the back of the church, Seth Fryer sensed that something he hadn't bargained for was afoot. For the first time, he noticed Grant and Kathryn Evans sitting near the front, and their companionship infuriated him. Sour hatred for the young railwayman twisted inside him, always had done since the abortive hanging had made him look a fool. The mother had rejected Fryer, now the daughter was turning to another man – and Grant at that!

Hendrix was continuing, the power in his voice increasing as he warmed to his subject.

'The devil I speak of is, at this very moment, amongst us as we go about our worship, masquerading as an angel of light. He knows the secret of the terrible event that has afflicted our community, and I speak of the disappearance of a lady we all respected and loved – Anne Evans. On his way to Barclay, my good friend, the Reverend Robert Cable, witnessed this monster of a man burying a body in the woods. The body was that of Anne Evans, a fact that I have since verified with my own eyes.'

Kathryn emitted a loud sob and Grant slipped his arm around her shoulder, trying to comfort her, wishing that the awful news could have been given to her in a gentler way.

But Hendrix was thundering on. 'In the Lord's name, I hereby accuse the devil who killed Anne Evans and tried to conceal her poor body. That devil is none other than our sheriff, Seth Fryer. He killed her—'

'*No!*' Seth Fryer's denial came like the roar of a beast, and all heads turned towards the back of the church.

Grant glanced over his shoulder, saw how the town sheriff had come to his feet, his face grey as he reared above those around him.

'It is true,' the Reverend Robert Cable was shouting. 'I saw it with my own eyes, and I will lead anybody to the grave and show them the body.'

Fryer, his face working with fury, had drawn his gun – the awesome Dragoon. One man stepped towards him, but he cuffed him across the side of the face with the barrel and the man went down with the sound of splintering pews. A woman screamed.

Hendrix shouted from his pulpit. 'Seth Fryer is guilty of this awful crime!'

At that moment Fryer fired his gun; the boom sounded deafening in the crowded church. The bullet, obviously intended for Hendrix, struck the edge of the pulpit and ricocheted to strike the surprised Robert Cable, splattering his blood all around. He was thrown back on to the boarded floor where he lay unmoving, most of his head blown away by the massive conical cartridge.

The congregation had erupted into turmoil, screaming and shouting, people standing up, struggling for space. Grant saw a fight going on at the back of the church. Seth Fryer was barging and kicking his way to the door, thrusting aside those in his way with his great arms. In the doorway, his hunched figure blocking the light, Fryer paused and swung around, his face contorted with hatred. He raised his gun, fired at Hendrix over the heads of the cowering congregation, but the bullet thundered wide, blowing the arm from a statue of Saint Peter.

The crush of pale-faced people seemed to clear from the aisle, the confusion gradually lessened, and Grant noticed that where Seth Fryer had previously been, there was now only empty doorway.

Grant ensured that Kathryn was unharmed, then he

pushed his way to the church entrance and gazed down the street. There was no sight of Seth Fryer, but as Grant gazed around he heard the beat of departing hoofs fading into the distance.

Sensing that he was trapped, Fryer had virtually admitted his guilt by his actions. Now he would roam free like a wild beast, holding the vulnerable town in a grip of terror. And there was no local law to deal with the threat.

The words of the mayor, Aaron Creswell, cut into the hysterical rabble. He was addressing Hendrix. 'Take us to where Mrs Evans is buried so we can see for ourselves.'

A muttering approval came from the men present. Hendrix was stooping over the prostrate body of Robert Cable and had been joined by Dr Carter. He rose to his feet, shaking his head.

'Sure, I'll do that.' His voice rang with a godlike righteousness. 'Then you will know the guilty devil that man is and you will seek him out and punish him!'

Grant felt Kathryn clinging to his arm. She was trembling violently.

'I must go as well,' she whispered. 'I must see her.'

'No,' he said firmly. 'Your mother's body, if it is hers, will be brought in and given a proper burial. You must let others do it.'

'But, Grant . . .'

'No,' he repeated firmly. She took a deep breath and accepted what he said.

As the exodus from the church took place and men went for their horses, Grant was tempted to join the party that was setting out, but suddenly he knew that there was a greater need for his presence elsewhere. There was no guarantee that Fryer had gone any distance. He was quite mad, that was evident, and had cloaked his evil for too long in a mantle of twisted virtuousness, revelling in the death of others. He could return at any time and inflict violence, and if Kathryn somehow crossed his path, she would pay the same penalty as her poor mother had done. Grant knew he must stay and protect her.

Most of the town's menfolk accompanied Mayor Creswell as he rode out of town, including the grim-faced Hendrix who was showing the way to the burial site. Of course it was possible that Seth Fryer was already there himself, digging up the remains in an effort to destroy the evidence, and that was why Hendrix urged the mayor to greater haste.

For the first time, men, including the former vigilantes, were standing up to Seth Fryer. For years they had cowered in fear in his intimidating presence, believing all he said. Now, everything had changed and they were given a sense of bravado by their numbers. Even Fryer could not fight off a score of well-armed men.

But the trouble was, they had to find him first. And Seth Fryer was not to be underestimated. Furthermore, he was as crafty as he was big.

SIXTEEN

The day's light was fading, the shadows purpled and flattened out, darkening the forested slopes adjacent to Pilgrim's Pinnacle. Some of the men, as they rode, recalled the last time they had hastened from the town, but then circumstances had been very different, for winter had blurred the landscape with ice and snow and Seth Fryer had been at their head, intent on introducing train-robbers to the lynching-rope. Now it was he who deserved no less. But the very knowledge that there was no telling where his formidable presence would next appear, had men glancing furtively around as they passed along the forested trails and between overhanging ridges.

The Reverend Benjamin Hendrix had no difficulty in finding the spot which the now deceased Clayton had shown him, but he approached it with caution, afraid that Fryer might be waiting to ambush them.

At the edge of the trees, the party dismounted, tethered their mounts and proceeded on foot, wishing that dusk hadn't taken such a firm hold. All sensed an eerie atmosphere, begrudging the crackle of twigs beneath their boots.

The grave remained as Hendrix had restored it and soon he and the mayor were digging at the soil, the latter breathing heavily, for he was unaccustomed to physical labour, being happier in the running of his bank or in his official mayoral duties. None the less, the two men presently put aside their spades and stooped to grope downward into the soil and drag out the blanket-wrapped bundle. The others grouped around them gasped as they realized that here was the corpse of Anne Evans.

But they were given no time to contemplate, for at that moment the night rocked with the blast of a gunshot, coming from the nearby trees, and before their eyes Aaron Creswell was knocked sideways, tumbling unceremoniously on to the ground, the stain of blood darkening his coat. Most men ducked down, taking what cover they could from the uneven ground in case another bullet came seeking a target. For a moment the only sound was that of ragged breathing and the groaning of Aaron Creswell who lay exposed across the piled earth that had been taken from the grave.

Abe Cromwell, the Barclay baker, suggested that they should go hunting for whoever had fired that shot. Nobody doubted it was Fryer. But the idea was rapidly rejected, what with night coming on and the prospect of coming face to face with a deranged killer.

Hendrix assumed a seemingly unnatural command of the situation, almost as if he was more accustomed to dealing with such matters than he was to conducting church services. He supervised the bandaging of Creswell's neck where the bullet had caught him. An inch further in and it would have killed him. Now he was gradually recovering from the shock of it. Hendrix then assisted him on to his horse. Finally, he had the body of Anne Evans gathered up, tied firm within its blanket, and fastened over his horse behind his saddle. The party delayed no longer, having little desire to remain in this rugged terrain with a maniac stalking them. They set off at a brisk pace, keeping alert.

The thoughts moiling in Hendrix's brain would have staggered his companions had they been revealed, for they were not of a godly nature. He was not dissatisfied with the day's events. Admittedly, he had lost his most loyal lieutenant, Frank Clayton, but he could be replaced, and with the threat of Seth Fryer's pseudo-law removed from Barclay, a bank robbery would prove easy pickings, but it would have to be carried out soon.

At the Evans home, Kathryn remained silent as she sat in the parlour. Beth Cromwell, a kindly soul, sat next to her on the sofa, busy with her knitting.

Kathryn gazed around at everything familiar and was tormented by the thought that this very room was where her mother had faced her ordeal. Grant did not disturb her, knowing there was little comfort he could bring. The hope was in him that the mayoral posse might return with a body that was not that of the girl's mother, but he did not mention this, not wishing to raise hopes that could be dashed.

Instead, he debated whether he should leave this girl, but the prospect of leaving her, despite the fact that she had Mrs Cromwell for company, did not appeal to him while her mother's murderer still roamed free.

121

Presently, Kathryn lit an oil-lamp and the graceful movement of her hands fascinated him. She pulled the curtains over.

'You should lie down,' he advised. 'If you want, I'll stay here tonight. I'll sleep in the chair.'

'Yes,' Kathryn said.

Mrs Cromwell gave them a surprised look, then nodded. 'I'll get Grant a blanket.' She went in the next room and he heard her open a cupboard, then she came back, handing him a folded blanket.

'Grant,' Kathryn said, 'do you think they'll want me to identify Ma's body? Tonight, I mean?'

'You get some rest,' he repeated. 'When they come back, I'll find out what's happening and let you know.'

'I'm very grateful, Grant.' She came to him, grasped his hand and gave it a squeeze. 'From the first time I saw you, when Joe brought you here, I knew you were a good man.' Making sure that Beth Cromwell was turned away, she touched his cheek with her lips and then went up the stairs to her room.

Shortly, Beth Cromwell wished him goodnight and went up the stairs.

Grant opened the front door, stepped out into the street, breathing in the cool air. The town appeared silent, bathed in moonlight. He wondered where Fryer was now – how far away, or how near. He shuddered. Until the man was killed or captured, nobody was safe.

It was another hour before Aaron Creswell, the Reverend Hendrix and their party returned, bearing the body of Anne Evans. Creswell immediately went to Dr Carter's surgery for his wound to be treated. Meanwhile, Hendrix handed over the corpse to the town's undertaker, and was discussing matters with him, when Grant entered. Hendrix felt his nerves tighten, but Grant showed no recognition of him. His recollections of the night before his attempted lynching seemed understandably vague.

Grant asked to see the corpse and the blanket was drawn back for his benefit. He winced at what he saw, but there was no doubt in his mind that his hopes of this not being Kathryn's mother were dashed. He was glad he had not mentioned that possibility to the girl.

'Seems as though she was strangled,' the undertaker commented as he allowed the blanket to fall back into place.

Grant nodded his thanks and departed, anxious not to leave Kathryn unprotected for any longer than necessary. Back at the house, he climbed carefully up the stairs. The door of Kathryn's room was half-open. As he stood on the small landing in the dim light coming up from downstairs, he heard the even sound of her breathing. And along with it came the sound of Beth Cromwell's snores. Both women were asleep and there was no point in waking them. He would tell Kathryn everything in the morning.

He returned to the parlour, ensured the front door was securely bolted, blew out the lamp and rested down in the chair, pulling the blanket over him. He had not carried a handgun for some time. He decided that from tomorrow he would have to be armed.

At last he slipped into troubled sleep, but suddenly he came awake, instinct warning him that something unnatural had disturbed him. The room was in total darkness and he strained his ears to catch any repetition of movement or sound. And then it came to him, borne along the town street by the night breeze. The clanging of the church bell. As he came to his feet, casting aside the blanket, the tolling sounded once more, then was silent.

Drawing wrappers over their nightdresses, both women had come down the stairs. Kathryn's voice startled him, 'What is it?'

'Wait here,' he said. 'Bolt the door after I've gone out.'

'Don't go,' she said.

'Something's wrong, Kathryn. I'll find out what it is. Remember, bolt the door and stay here.'

Once outside, he waited until he heard the door made secure, then he walked along the sidewalk towards the church. The moon had gone now and he figured it was maybe three or four o'clock. As he went, he was aware that other men had stepped out from their houses. Somebody said, 'What the hell is that church bell ringing for at this time of night, disturbing folks? Has the reverend gone plumb crazy?'

Another voice responded: 'Well, we better find out, but keep your eyes peeled in case Fryer's loitering around! I don't fancy getting shot again.'

Grant realized it was Aaron Creswell speaking and, glancing around, he saw the whiteness of the man's bandage showing in the gloom. Soon the group had joined forces, swelled by others, most still in their nightshirts, and together they approached the shadowy church, apprehension reflected in their hushed voices.

To their surprise, the door stood open, but there was no light from within. Grant was first inside. He

124

extracted a block of matches from his pocket and struck a light and held it up. Everybody peered into the church.

Suddenly breaths were exhaled in horror. '*My God, no!*' Stumpy Simmons cried out.

Gently swinging, a body was suspended on the bell rope just inside the door, the neck extended, the ghastly, contorted face painted orange in the glow of sulphur. The match burned Grant's fingers and went out and they were plunged into darkness. But the vision had been branded into their minds.

What they'd seen was the body of the Reverend Benjamin Hendrix, suspended on his own bell-rope, his head twisted at an unnatural angle by the knot at his neck, his toes just a couple of feet above the floor. In the confusion, somebody blundered against him, causing the body to sway, bringing a tentative ring from the bell.

'Lynched,' Grant gasped, 'lynched by his own bell-rope!'

'Fryer must've done it, no doubt about that,' Creswell remarked. 'But where's he now!'

For a moment they stood in uncertainty, some shivering as they wondered. In their minds, Fryer had assumed the proportions of a behemoth.

At last Cromwell spoke, his voice tremulous. 'Hiding up some place, getting ready to strike again.'

Somebody had now found a lamp and put a match to its wick. Men peered around nervously in the gloom, straining their ears, but the only sound they heard was breeze whispering through the eaves.

Creswell had Hendrix's body cut down, and for a

moment they all stood around, sickened by what had happened. This man had been a respected member of their society, had indeed brought comfort to many in his pastoral role. Had the truth been known of the other side to Hendrix's life, feelings would have been very different, but for now the only sentiments were of grief – and fear as to where the killer would strike again.

At last the mayor's eyes fell upon Grant. 'You stood for the post of sheriff,' he said. 'The election of Seth Fryer proved to be the biggest mistake this town has ever made. The job's yours if you'll take it on. We need law in Barclay, to make it safe and rid us of this terror.'

From all around came grunts of agreement. 'Yeah, sure. We need you now, Grant.'

Suddenly there was a scurrying sound from the roof of the church and everybody flinched with alarm – and relaxed.

'Damned crows on the roof,' Abe Cromwell murmured.

'Don't curse in a church,' Creswell reprimanded him, and turned again towards Grant.'Will you take the job on?'

Grant swallowed hard. The demands of town sheriff had increased considerably since he'd last put himself forward. He was aware of his limitations. He looked at the pale faces surrounding him, all awaiting his response with breath-held intensity. He thought of Kathryn, alone, vulnerable in her house, waiting for news of events, and of Fryer somewhere out there, more dangerous, more insane, than ever.

At last he nodded and mouthed a soft, 'Yes, I'll take the job,' and Creswell exhaled with relief.

Soon, they were busy removing the corpse to the overworked mortuary.

SEVENTEEN

Along with Beth Cromwell, Kathryn was waiting in the parlour when he returned. Both women wept as he confirmed, as gently as he could, that the body to which the Reverend Hendrix had led them had been Anne's. He then related the astounding events that had followed and Kathyrn shuddered at the thought of Fryer taking his vengeance in such an evil way. Presently she dried her eyes and he saw something else in her then, something beyond the need to grieve – a hard edge that would not submit to threat.

She said, 'He's got to be stopped, before he does more harm.'

Grant nodded, conscious that the man's next targets could well be the girl – and himself.

'They asked me to take over as town sheriff,' he said, 'and I agreed. I'll buy a gun in the morning. Can't have a lawman going round unarmed, especially now.'

She looked at him with wide, concerned eyes. 'You must be careful,' she murmured.

After Beth Cromwell had returned to bed, anticipating that the girl would follow, Kathryn slipped her arms around him, rested her head on his chest and whispered, 'I couldn't stand it if anything happened to you.'

He smoothed her auburn hair, knowing that he was being drawn deeper into a relationship with this girl, and not regretting it.

She made some coffee and they spent what was left of that eventful night sitting at the parlour table. He tried to draw her thoughts away from her tragedies by telling her about his own life, and how his wife Josephine had been taken ill and died; how he had quit Texas and come north, anxious to start a new life. How events had taken a horrifying turn when he had spotted the ruptured rail-line. As he mentioned Joe, her brother, and the way he had helped him, she lowered her head, and he regretted giving her renewed sadness, but shortly she faced him again and said, 'Go on.'

She noticed how he rubbed his neck. She knew it pained him, yet he never complained.

He told her everything, apart from about the distressing occasion when Hugo Eriksson had come home unexpectedly. He grimaced at the thought. He comforted himself with the assurance that Kathryn need never be aware of his shame.

Shortly after dawn, Beth Cromwell prepared breakfast, and as they cleared away the pots, Mayor Creswell called, still looking dazed from events and troubled by his wound. Kathryn accepted Creswell's condolences graciously and brought him coffee.

'A brave girl, Kathryn Evans is,' he commented as she returned to the kitchen.

He'd brought Grant a shield-shaped sheriff's badge. He slid it across the table and said, 'We're all relying on you, Grant. The whole town will be in jitters until Fryer is destroyed. You'll no doubt want to move into the sheriff's office as soon as possible.'

Grant nodded, although he didn't relish the prospect of moving into the office where so recently Fryer had ruled the roost. He felt overwhelmed at the confidence that was being placed in him, despite the fact that he was completely untested so far as the town was concerned. Everybody was desperate, anxious to hang their hope on any available hook – and there was no one else willing to take the job on, not with a ready-made adversary lusting to kill you.

Creswell stayed for half an hour, then departed to open up his bank. Grant penned a letter to the railroad, tendering his resignation and walked to the station to have it sent up the line.

As the day's heat began to take hold, Kathryn accompanied him to the town gunsmith's where he pondered over a selection of guns before a Navy Colt caught his eye. He hefted the weapon, opened the loading-gate and gave the cylinder a twirl. The gun was not new, but its parts were well maintained and oiled. He nodded his approval and bought some ammunition, loading five cartridges. He next chose a leather holster and strapped it on. He had no great love for guns, but he had developed skills when he had been a deputy down in Texas, though he had always been conscious that many men had a greater aptitude for gun-play than he did.

Next, they went to the newly erected sheriff's office. It was a two-storey log building, well-built and boasting two iron-barred cells. The upper floor, with its living accommodation, was reached by outside stairs.

They spent an hour sorting through Fryer's belongings, clearing his desk and drawers, but there was little of a personal nature, even in the upstairs room, and what there was they boxed away. The only thing they found to remind them of the man's wicked nature were some dozen ropes, neatly coiled and stacked in the corner, and instinct told Grant that these were the ropes that Fryer had used to lynch men and that he had kept them as mementoes. Grant wondered if the rope with which his attempted lynching had been affected was amongst them, and he shuddered at the thought and had no desire to reintroduce himself to those strands. Whether Kathryn realized what the ropes represented, he was uncertain, but they left them where they were, untouched.

Grant found a list of the men who had acted as vigilantes, and he worked out a roster of guard duties and patrols of the town that he considered appropriate, night and day. The last thing he wanted was for Fryer to slip back into Barclay and create more havoc. When he was finished, he pinned up the roster on the outside notice board, then they locked the office and turned their attention to the next matter in hand – checking out the church.

Grant was glad enough that Kathryn remained with him. He was constantly aware that she would be at great risk. Fryer could be lurking anywhere, even within the town, waiting his chance to strike, and in consequence Grant remained watchful, keeping upper-floor windows and even roofs under scrutiny as they passed along.

The town was making a brave attempt to resume normal life; the stores and saloon were open, trains and stagecoaches remained on schedule, but there was a marked absence of folks on the street and those who were about appeared furtive. All acknowledged Grant as they saw him, glad enough that somebody had enough courage to take over Fryer's badge and defend them against evil.

The church appeared tranquil, its main door still open. It had been the scene of incredible violence of late, blood had stained its floor, two men had met terrible deaths and nobody had returned since the discovery of the reverend's body.

It would have been easy for Fryer to enter the church unseen. He had probably been awaiting Hendrix on his return from leading the posse to the body of Anne Evans, waiting with his heart full of hatred for the man who had revealed his guilt and rendered him an outcast.

Apprehensively, Grant and Kathryn stepped inside, their eyes gradually adjusting to the dimness after the brightness of the sun.

'This church will have to be reconsecrated,' Grant said, 'before folks can come here without thinking about the killings.'

Kathryn nodded. 'What are you going to do, Grant?'

'Oh, we'll check it to make sure all is well, then make it as secure as we can. It will have to stay locked up until a new minister can be found.'

But what he'd imagined would be a sad but routine job, took on a very different mantle when they stepped into the little office at the back. It was here that Hendrix had his desk. A casual examination of the drawers had Grant exclaiming his amazement.

The first indication that all was not as he'd anticipated came when he found his railway cap, the one that
had been stolen from him during his encounter with
that outlaw after the posse had jumped the train-
robbers, and that was only the start of amazing revela-
tions. Correspondence was found – letters written in
the illiterate hands of men who operated on the wrong
side of the law, giving ideas for prospective robberies.
Hardly believing what he was uncovering, Grant found
maps of the railroad, with markings to indicate where
hold-ups could be effected. A whole armoury of guns
was discovered in a back cupboard, totally beyond
anything that a humble minister might require. Further
incriminating evidence was found in the saddlebags of
the so-called Reverend Robert Cable – decidedly non-
clerical clothing, a large bandanna, well-used hand-
guns, roughly scrawled maps of banks and railroads,
and a letter from Hendrix, addressed to Cable's real
name, Frank Clayton, asking him to come to Barclay as
he had certain plans in mind which would prove highly
profitable.

Grant knew that the federal authorities must be
given this information. Information that clearly
revealed the criminal activity that had taken place in
the territory.

After Grant informed the mayor of his findings,
Creswell checked for himself and that very same day a
special edition of the town newspaper was published,
detailing the appalling events and emerging revela-
tions. Incredulous tongues were soon spreading the
news far and wide. And a different style of burying was
arranged for the falsely respected minister. Now, he

would be laid to rest in a far corner of the cemetery, along with the so-called Reverend Robert Cable, and their epitaphs would indicate the scoundrels they had been.

EIGHTEEN

Two days later, Grant took the train to Catto, collected
his belongings from his lodgings, paid his dues to Mrs
Tolly and returned to Barclay. By the evening he had
moved into the room above the town sheriff's office,
glad that Beth Cromwell was still staying with Kathryn.
Furthermore, he was satisfied that the patrolling former
vigilantes would obey his instructions to pay particular
attention to Kathryn's safety and to let him know immediately anything untoward occurred.

He had thought long and hard about his future.
Everything hinged around his ability to destroy Seth
Fryer, and he knew that if he failed to do this, Fryer
would not let matters rest. The man's obsession with
death was both unnatural and unnerving. It was an
eerie feeling, now occupying the very place where Fryer
had existed. Grant tried to remove every trace of the
man's existence from the building, even slinging those
grim ropes into the yard at the back, but Fryer's evil
presence somehow continued to pervade the air.

There was something else on Grant's mind. The
longer he spent with Kathryn as his companion, the
more he became impressed with the girl's courage and

her gentle, sweet nature. Since Josephine's death, he had doubted that he would ever marry again, but now his ideas were changing. There was no comparison between Josephine and Kathryn. They were quite different, each with their own merits, but he was finding that his earlier protective, almost fatherly, attitude towards Kathryn was changing, and he was seeing her as the young, attractive woman she was. He had no doubt that Kathryn was equally drawn to him, that he was not just an assumed bastion of strength she would ultimately tire of. And the knowledge gave him a sensation of longing inside.

Three days later they stood side by side amongst a sizeable gathering of townsfolk as her mother was laid to rest in the cemetery, her grave alongside that of her son Joe, no reference being made as to the hateful way that each had met their end. There being no minister to officiate, Mayor Creswell conducted the short service, leading the hymns and reading from the Bible: *The Lord is my shepherd* . . . Afterwards, there was a brief wake in the saloon.

Presently, as the assembly drifted back out into the street, they all heard the long whistle of a locomotive signalling 'down brakes' as a train from Catto pulled into the station. Grant and Kathryn were lingering on the boardwalk outside the saloon, talking to some of the other mourners, as a few passengers dismounted and came down the street. Out of habit, Grant glanced at them to make sure that none posed a threat. Then suddenly his heart dipped into his boots. A woman was approaching, rushing along in a harassed manner, her bosom bouncing with the exertion, her low-cut red

dress drawing glances. He remembered how her probing hands had plucked the turkey. It was Laura
Eriksson. He had hoped he would never set eyes on her
again.

Shrinking into the shadows beneath the saloon
balcony, he saw her pause as she encountered a man
walking in the opposite direction, his uncertain steps
indicating that he recently imbibed hard liquor. Her
high-pitched question sounded clearly in the still
evening air. 'Excuse me, sir. Can you tell me where I can
find Grant Mayo, please?'

'Why yes, ma'am,' the man responded and waved his
arm towards the saloon, too taken aback to comment
further.

Laura's sharp eyes found Grant immediately, making
his retreat impracticable, and she rushed towards him,
raising her skirt above her booted ankles as she
mounted the steps to the boardwalk.

'Grant,' she gasped, 'I'm so relieved to find you.
I . . .' at last she glanced around at the other people
watching her, all of them dressed in the blackest of
funeral clothes. She seemed to debate whether to
continue or not, then apparently decided to throw
caution to the winds, albeit dropping her voice down a
notch or two, ensuring that ears were perked up even
higher to catch her words. 'I've left Hugo. I can't stand
being penned up in that chicken-coop of a shack any
longer. I . . . I need to talk to you, Grant – desperately.
You're the only person I . . .'

Grant held up his hand to silence her, aware of the
surprised expressions of those around him. His neck
was tingling with embarrassment.

'We better go across to my office,' he said, and he nodded an apology to his companions, including Kathryn whose horrified look blazed at him indignantly. But he took Laura's arm and shepherded her across the street to his office. Once inside, he sat her down and slid behind his desk, not wishing to prolong the conversation any more than was necessary.

She was gazing around with incredulous eyes at the office and at his badge. 'So you're town sheriff, Grant. Well, my oh my.'

'Laura,' he said, 'why have you come here?'

She assumed a hurt, little girl look. 'I couldn't stand it any longer, Grant. I mean there in the shack and Hugo away so much. And I kept remembering how it was between us. You know at Christmas time when . . .'

'Yes,' he interrupted, 'I'll never forget.'

'Me neither,' she sighed. 'Well, it was only right that I should find you. I kinda hoped we could carry on where we left off, honey.'

He rose to his feet, peered over the top of the lace curtain and across the street. The group outside the saloon had dispersed, including Kathryn. He swung back.

'That's all in the past, Laura. I was grateful to you and Hugo for all your kindness, and I felt really bad about what happened, but . . .'

She looked exasperated. 'There was no need to feel bad, Grant. It just reminded me of how good things could be. You see Hugo got wounded during the war. It kinda . . . well it affected him so he couldn't love a woman like most men can, like a woman expects.'

He nodded.

138

'I guess you never really understood what Hugo explained that night,' she went on. 'He knew I wanted a baby more than anything else in the whole world, still do. And he said that as he couldn't do the job himself, then you would be sure to breed sound stock. The only problem was he came back too soon. He'd forgotten what we'd arranged.'

'Laura,' he said firmly, 'I'm going to marry a lady called Kathryn Evans. I love her a lot and I don't want anything to spoil that.'

'Oh glory!' she gasped. 'I . . . I don't want to upset things for you, though I was hoping we could be together. Maybe just one more time.'

'I'm sorry,' he said. 'I can't help you, Laura. You best stay in Barclay tonight. I'll book a room for you at the hotel.'

Her face was a picture of misery and tears glistened on her cheeks.

He stood up, helped her from her chair. He gave her his handkerchief to dry her eyes. As they stepped outside into the warm evening and he led her up the street to the hotel, she murmured, 'I suppose I've made a fool of myself.'

They walked for a moment and he wondered how Hugo would accept her running out on him. He'd always had the feeling that the Swede loved his wife, despite their differences.

At the hotel, he booked a room for her, and the clerk handed her the key with a wry smile. She was reluctant to leave Grant, her eyes still tearful. She held his hand for a long moment, then she leaned forward and kissed him on the cheek before turning away.

Grant left the hotel, his thoughts turning to Kathryn. He felt bad about her and wondered what conclusions she'd reached regarding this intrusive woman. He debated whether or not to visit her and explain the situation, but as he stood outside his office, feeling the heat and dust brought by a gusty wind, he heard a shout and down the otherwise deserted street he saw a man beckoning frantically. As he ran towards him he caught the gist of his words.

'Fire, Sheriff . . . over at Rokers'!'

Smoke was already tainting the air. Grant recalled that Roker owned a small ranch just beyond the eastern side of town and as he glanced upward he saw dark smoke blowing across the sky. He met Stumpy Simmons, the man who had been so helpful to Seth Fryer at the time of Grant's 'lynching', but he held no resentment now. He sent him scurrying away with instructions to spread word of the fire.

Soon, men were hurrying to the scene of the conflagration. Flame licked through the timber ranch house, made tinder-dry by the recent drought. Fortunately the Roker couple with their four children had escaped to safety. It was obvious that little could be done to save their residence, but townsfolk worked by passing buckets of water along a chain. Grant toiled, supervising the bringing out of horses from the stable, setting free the hogs as the wind bore flame and choking smoke too close for comfort. Mayor Creswell, despite his bandaged arm, and other members of the town council did their best to contain the fire, saying that it was on the agenda of their next committee meeting to set up a local fire brigade. This might have been quite helpful if the fire had started a month later.

Will Roker, between wringing his hands in despair and cursing, spoke of how a draught had blown over an oil-lantern, setting some curtains ablaze, and how there was nothing he could do to stop the flames sweeping from room to room.

Grant, and nigh all the menfolk of Barclay, worked hard that night, their faces blackened by smoke, and it was not until the small hours that everything had been dampened down and the fire no longer threatened. The Roker family had been given sanctuary by friends and what animal stock there was was made secure.

It was not long before dawn that Grant eventually returned to his room, and he was glad enough to take to his bed. It was 9.30 by the time he got up next morning and, after a wash and quick breakfast, he decided to visit Kathryn and explain the circumstances surrounding Laura Erickson. The recollection of Kathryn's shocked expression still haunted him.

But when he reached her house, it was Beth Cromwell who opened up. She said, 'If you're looking for Kathryn, she caught the nine o'clock stage to Miles City. She said she'd received a telegram saying her aunt had been taken ill.'

'Did she say anything else?' Grant enquired.

'Nothing at all, Sheriff, though she seemed downright upset. Is the fire all out now? I'm sure feeling sorry for those poor Roker folk, losing their home and all.'

He nodded his shared concern, but his main worries involved Kathryn. Had it really been her aunt's ill health that had caused her to leave town so suddenly, or had the visit of Laura Erickson triggered off some emotion, some hurt, in her that had sent her scurrying away?

He felt uneasy about her. He had no way to tell how long she would be away. Perhaps she would telegraph him . . . or perhaps she would not, leaving him to this woman from his past. Apart from any bruised feelings that she might have, he knew that she would be defenceless if Fryer learned that he was no longer acting as her personal bodyguard.

He returned to his office, sat behind his desk and knew that he would have to take action. But the trouble was, he had no idea where Fryer was. Grant had telegraphed surrounding law agencies informing them of how dangerous the man was, but there were plenty of places he could go where he would not be recognized. On the other hand, he might still be lurking in the hills surrounding Barclay, keeping watch on the town, planning where next to strike.

He tried to shrug off the feeling, but it persisted. He felt the main target for Fryer's vengeance would now be himself. He had always held a grudge, ever since he'd been made to look foolish at lynching the wrong man, but now his hatred would be even more intensified by jealousy at the way Grant had taken over his job as sheriff.

While Fryer was free and armed, Grant knew that he would have to be constantly alert. No doubt while the town was patrolled by ex-vigilante deputies, Barclay remained his safest place, but night and day patrols by volunteers could not be maintained indefinitely. The good will the ex-vigilantes felt towards their new sheriff, their remorse at having nigh lynched him, would surely wear thin.

That day the heat was stifling, borne on a relentless breeze that brought dust and tumbleweed along the street and sucked moisture from the land. Grant checked the post office several times in case a telegram had come for him from Miles City, but the clerk shook his head. He wished he could have sent a telegram to Kathryn, at her aunt's, but he did not have the address. As the long, listless hours dragged by, his anxiety increased. He gazed out at the surrounding hills, wondering if, even at this moment, Fryer was watching the town.

And then, come evening, the telegraph lines buzzed, and the clerk appeared waving a message for the sheriff. As Grant scanned the wording, the blood drained from his face.

STAGE FROM BARCLAY TO MILES CITY HELD UP AT GUN POINT BY MASKED MAN NEAR WILLARD'S CROSSING STOP MISS KATHRYN EVANS ABDUCTED.

NINETEEN

He was frantic with concern. There was no doubt in his mind who the 'masked man' was. Clearly, Seth Fryer had spied out on Barclay from the nearby hills, spotted the girl take the stage – and seen his chance. With Kathryn at his mercy, there was no telling how long she would survive, and what gruesome torment was being inflicted upon her. Perhaps she was already dead. Grant knew that he would have to ride out and hunt Fryer down, but, if Kathryn still survived, she would be a helpless pawn in a game of life and death.

Grant hastened to discuss matters with Mayor Creswell who suggested leading a party of deputies out, but Grant shook his head.

'Too risky,' he said. 'Fryer could watch us from the time we left town and pick us off one by one. I don't want to push him into doing anything drastic to Kathryn.' He shook his head with the misery he felt, blaming himself for leaving her alone. If only Laura Erickson had not shown up in town. If only the Roker fire hadn't occupied him all night.

Creswell took his handkerchief out and mopped his

brow. He was as much at a loss as to the best action to take as Grant was.

'I hope he's kidnapped her to use as a hostage,' Grant said. 'That being so, at least she'll still be alive. But the man's so evil, so depraved, there's no telling what he'll do to her.' He tried to draw his thoughts together, to bring some coherence to his reasoning. 'I'll have to go out and find him.'

Creswell frowned. 'He'll ambush you.'

'I'll wait till dark,' Grant said. 'Come dawn, I'll be hidden up some place. Maybe I can spy out where he's holding her.'

Creswell nodded reluctantly. Neither man was at all confident at the prospect, but there seemed little alternative. Both Fryer and the girl could be miles away by now.

Grant stepped down from the mayor's veranda and was walking back to his office when he noticed a single rider approaching along the street, riding so slowly he scarcely raised the dust. As the man drew closer, it was evident that he was in a sorry state, his clothing being in tatters and his mare worn down. When he drew rein, his beast needed no second invitation to stop. He took a flask from his pocket, uncorked it and pressed it to his lips for a swig. Finding it less full than he'd hoped, he cursed and nudged his mare into shuffling motion again. Outside the sheriff's office, he stopped again and half-fell from his saddle. He was gaining no response from his knocking on the office door when Grant's approach from behind him made him jump with alarm. He turned, his wizened face, a weather-beaten network of wrinkles, registering relief as he noticed the lawman's badge.

'Sheriff Mayo?' he enquired, and on Grant's confirmation he extracted a crumpled envelope from his pocket. 'Met this fella on the trail,' he said. 'He was the biggest man I ever saw, like a great bear. He told me to give this to you, that you'd set me up right well with whiskey.'

Agitation was surging through Grant as he tore the envelope open, immediately recognizing the bold handwriting, having seen other examples in the office, as that of Seth Fryer!

Mayo
I'm tired of being a pariah, stuck out here in the wild, but at least I'm no longer alone, having this pretty young lady for company. I don't know why I've been treated so bad, after all the service I did the town. Furthermore, there's no proof I've done any bad things, nothing that would stand up in a court of law. That's why I need to talk with you, negotiate some sort of arrangement. We can let bygones be bygones. What I want is for us to meet and talk things through, and I suggest you come to the old miner's cabin at the western end of Webber's Canyon at noon on Friday – just you and nobody else. If you try any fancy tricks, I'll have no option but to make the girl suffer, and that's a promise. I repeat: come alone and come unarmed, then maybe I'll release her. But remember, tell nobody about this and play it square. That way, I may let you have her back.
Seth Fryer

Grant felt the blood throbbing in his temples. His mind was so focused that he forgot the scarecrow who'd delivered the message until he coughed.

'Where was it that the big man gave you this?' Grant enquired.

'Along the Catto trail, 'bout a mile from here. He came riding out of the trees and blocked my way. Didn't seem the sort of fella to pick an argument with.'

Grant expressed his gratitude, reached into his pocket and passed over a dollar. The man's eyes lit up, and there was a new spark to his movements as he led his mare over to the saloon, hitched her to the rail and disappeared through the batwings.

It was now noon on Wednesday. That meant Grant had forty-eight hours till the proposed meeting with Fryer. He didn't trust Fryer one iota, but, in the interests of Kathryn's safety, he had to appear to comply with everything the man demanded.

He penned a letter for the mayor, explaining what had happened, sealed it and wrote on the envelope beneath the mayor's name: *Please do not open till Friday noon.* He would leave it prominently displayed on his desk.

He had no intention of meeting Fryer unarmed. He would hide the Navy Colt beneath his shirt and slip a knife into his boot-top.

Wednesday afternoon dragged by, the heat reducing activity in the town to the minimum. The surrounding hills shimmered in the sun's searing rays. In the evening, Grant patrolled the sidewalks, exchanging greetings with acquaintances, checking to make certain all was well, but he suspected it was unlikely that Fryer would play his hand prior to the proposed meeting on Friday. Grant knew the spot he'd mentioned: Webber's Canyon. The railroad tracks ran along it for maybe ten miles before branching off towards Catto. He'd never followed it further, but he would make sure he found the old miner's cabin.

Continuing with his evening patrol, he eventually reached the railroad station and along the platform, waiting for the next train, he spotted Hugo and Laura Erickson. Surprisingly, their arms were linked and Grant smiled to himself, grateful that they appeared to have settled their differences. He turned back into the town, having no wish to intrude into their freshly found closeness. He wondered what Hugo had promised her.

But any relief he'd felt at their apparent reconciliation was soon countered by grim thoughts of Kathryn's circumstances. What brutality had been inflicted upon her?

He spent a restless night, tormented by images of the girl's plight. Had Fryer ravaged her young body? Or had he killed her already and was bluffing to lure Grant to his death? The moment of truth would come at noon on Friday.

Somehow he got through the following day, counting each dragging hour. He did not sleep at all that night, just listened to the tick of his clock. He had saddled his piebald and was riding out before dawn on Friday morning, wondering if he was already under Fryer's distant observation, even maybe within the sights of his rifle. But he tried to divert his thoughts from himself, and dwell upon Kathryn and the state she must be in.

Around him, the morning's heat rose, the sky unbroken blue, the dust from his piebald's hoofs hanging in the air as he followed the little-used trail. Everywhere seemed misleadingly normal, with chipmunks pausing as they scurried along the branches to stare at him, the birds trilling brightly in the trees and crickets whirring in the grass. He even spotted a coyote in the fringe of the forest, giving him a long look, nostrils flared, before being absorbed back into the wild. In the distance, the railroad glistened in the sun and presently a freight train puffed westward towards Catto.

Pausing by a stream, he rolled and smoked a cigarette to steady the nervous tingle that was in him. A wood thrush skimmed past him and perched on a cottonwood branch above his head, viewing him with curiosity. He took out Fryer's note, read it through again, seeking some hidden meaning, but there was nothing to enlighten him. It was couched as almost a plea for help, albeit tinged with threats.

Come 10.30, he had left the railroad and swung deeper into Webber's Canyon, the air aromatic from lilac-berried junipers. On either side, bronzed boulders built up into soaring cliffs. He felt sure that he would see no more human life until he found, please God, Kathryn – and Seth Fryer, if he could be classed as human.

An hour later he made it to the western end of the canyon, its deep red walls broken by ridges and slopes. He had halted on the shoulder of a pine-cloaked ridge to gaze downward at the undulating meadow that formed the base of the canyon. Now, with the redolence of pine-needle and balsam in his nostrils, everywhere seemed unnaturally quiet, the only sound coming from birds fluttering in the branches above. He soon spotted the small, windowless shack, now half-hidden by encroaching weeds, close to the far wall of the canyon. There was no sign of life or movement, and he wondered if Fryer had lured him here for reasons other than the obvious. He scanned the surrounding trees and scrub and the rocky ledges above the shack, saw nothing untoward. Where was Kathryn? Apprehension knotted his stomach and he shivered despite the heat.

He smoked another cigarette, and when it was a stub he cast it aside, then he tethered the piebald and went forward on foot, his gaze focused on the shack, fully aware that he might be edging towards a death-trap. But he knew he could do nothing now but play along with Fryer's demands.

Within yards of the silent shack, he reassured himself with the feel of the Navy Colt hidden beneath his shirt. He undid a button, so that he could grasp the weapon quickly if needed. He glanced behind, attempting to assure himself that he was not about to be shot in the back. Pacing forward, he was aware of the sweat trickling down his body and the dull throb of the ever-present neck-pain.

The door of the shack had long rotted away, leaving an ugly black hole as the entrance. The place smelt of decay. He braced himself, reached the doorway and peered inside. At first, after the brightness of the sun, he saw nothing but gloom. Then, as he stood tensed for action, his eyes adjusted and he glimpsed a slight movement at the back end of the shack. Realization dawned on him. Kathryn was sitting on a chair, ropes encircling her, a gag over her mouth, the whites of her eyes striving to pass some message to him that she was otherwise helpless to impart.

Foolishly, his relief at finding her had him rushing towards her. It was then that the floor gave way beneath him and he plunged downward. In that second, he reached out, desperately striving to arrest his fall. His grip clutched around something solid, but there was no time to realize what it was as he dropped.

He thumped into soggy, clinging mud, with something heavy crunching on top of him with an impact that drove the breath from his body, left him teetering on the brink of unconsciousness. And then the groan came and he realized he was not alone. Still stunned, he pushed his hands out and made a startling discovery, for he touched the softness of a human body and then the solidity of wood – the chair!

In falling, he'd reached out and grabbed the leg of the chair and in so doing dragged the girl into this foul hole. Being bound, the only thing which had broken her fall had been his own body. As he dragged in a breath, he felt agony shoot through his ribs. But now his concern centred on the girl. As his senses clarified, he murmured her name, hearing only her groan as a response.

He tried to reason out what had happened. Clearly, he had fallen foul of Fryer's trap. How foolish he had been to blunder into it the way he had. The floor of the shack must have been covered with grass and weeds, concealing what so obviously was a deep well-shaft. He sighed with anguish.

He tried to raise himself from the evil-smelling ooze,

suddenly aware of the fact that in addition to the stink of rotting, stagnant vegetation and mud, another smell was permeating what air there was – kerosene. Desperation prevented him from reasoning further. His time might be limited. Unsure whether Kathryn was conscious or not, badly injured or not, he fumbled in the darkness, located the gag around her mouth. With frantic fingers, he tore at the knot and at last loosened it. As he pulled it free, she unleashed a great sigh of relief and groaned his name. 'Grant . . . how. . . ?'

He hushed her to silence, reaching down to extract the knife from his boot-top. Working blindly, striving to avoid cutting her, he somehow severed the bonds around her wrists and ankles, then he unwound the rope from her waist and she slumped free of the chair.

They were both panting with their efforts.

'Kathryn,' he gasped, 'are you badly hurt?'

'I'm still alive,' she whispered, 'and that's a miracle. I knew where the well was . . . that he'd covered it over . . . but there was nothing I could do to warn you.'

'Where is he now?' he asked.

Even had she known, there was no time to answer. The ground seemed to creak as a heavy weight moved across the floor above them, then came the sound of something being dragged over the opening high above their heads, increasing still further the lack of air within the shaft.

'He's blocked the top of the well,' Grant gasped.

'It's too high for us to climb up, anyway,' she groaned, 'and the walls are all slimy.'

For a moment they clung to each other in silence, he aware of the pain in his ribs and the fluttering beat of

152

her heart. Breathing in their kerosene-tainted prison was becoming increasingly difficult.

It came to Grant now, how the mere shooting of somebody was not enough for Fryer. Perhaps not even lynching gave him sufficient satisfaction. The man's lust for death had gone further than that, demanding new methods with more suffering. Grant felt his flesh crawl and his temples throbbed. With the smell of kerosene so overpowering, Fryer's intentions seemed increasingly clear. *He was going to cook them alive!*

His voice, sounding muffled, came to them through the covering he had pulled across. 'Kathryn, I never intended you to fall down there. It was only him I wanted. You know that! I'll get you out.'

Kathryn roused herself, the tension running through her, 'I'll not come out without Grant,' she cried. 'Kill us both if you have to.'

They heard him growl in exasperation, then shouted, 'Damn you! I'll come back!' and they heard him stomp out of the shack.

Gritting his teeth against the pain, Grant disentangled himself from Kathryn's arms, forced himself up. The ooze gripped his feet, making sucking sounds as he moved them. He reached up, wishing there was light to see, but all he could feel were the damp, slippery walls curving around them. Gradually his eyes became accustomed to the gloom, and far above his head he could see the slimmest chink of light. He knew that, despite his six-foot height, he would never be able to reach it.

A thought loomed in his mind. 'Kathryn, why is he so anxious for you to survive?'

He heard her sigh anxiously. 'He told me something I didn't believe.'

'What?'

'He told me that he wished me no harm. That he would kill everybody else in the world before he killed me. He told me that after my father died, he helped my mother face up to her bereavement and they became very close.'

'I bet she didn't feel that way,' he murmured.

'He told me if I checked my father's death certificate, I would find it dated a year before my birth . . .'

Grant allowed his brain to absorb her words, then he voiced his disbelief. 'You mean, he's your father!'

He heard her sob. 'So he says, Grant, so he says. And Joe's too.'

'Oh, God!'

'He said he always wanted to tell me, to love me, but my mother shut him out, refusing to have any more to do with him. He told me he never wanted to kill Joe, but the bullet ricocheted.'

Grant slumped back down. He could hardly believe his ears. 'So he kidnapped you to . . .'

'To get me back,' she murmured. 'To tell me everything.'

'So, he hasn't ill treated you?'

'Not until he tied me to the chair, and then he said it was just to lure you into this trap. I pleaded with him not to do it, but . . .' her voice gave out in a little choke of misery.

'You must get out of this place,' he gasped. 'There's no point in both of us dying.'

'I'll not leave you, Grant.'

154

'He'll be back soon. Do as I say, Kathryn. You must climb on my shoulders, try to reach up.'

'But, Grant . . .'

Anger put an edge on his voice. 'For God's sake, don't argue.'

He reached out, grabbed her by the shoulders and hoisted her on to his bent knee. Then he straightened up, suppressing a groan as she pulled herself over his ribs, got her knees on to his shoulders and then straightened up, bracing herself against the encircling wall. He could feel the increased weight forcing his feet deeper into the mire.

Her voice came down to him. 'I can't reach the top.'

He groaned with disappointment, but then another idea came to him. 'Come back down,' he said. 'I'll stand on the chair. That'll give us extra height.'

'Oh God!'

She slithered back down him, tumbling the last part, but she scrambled up immediately and located the chair. After they had placed it upright, they repeated the painful process of climbing upward. As Grant took the strain of her weight, he felt the chair sinking into the mud and was about to despair, when he felt the downward pressure of her feet lifted from his shoulders. She had hooked her fingers over the rim of the well-top, forcing back the planking Fryer had drawn across.

Thrusting her feet against the shaft wall, she struggled to gain purchase, almost lost her hold but somehow hung on. Seconds later, she drew her knee up and hoisted herself out, collapsing with exhaustion amid the weeds on the shack's earth floor.

It was then that Fryer's deep voice sounded. He'd been watching her all along. 'Saved me a job, you have!'

She lifted her head to see his great bulk silhouetted in the doorway, the rope he'd intended to drag her out with coiled over his shoulder. She slumped back down, dying a small death.

He held something up – a block of matches. 'Nice little trap I made, and he fell for it like the simpleton he is. One flame into that well and he'll be reduced to a cinder.' He allowed himself a mirthless laugh. 'Unless . . .' He left the word hanging.

'Unless what?' she gasped.

'Unless you come with me and behave like the true daughter you are. Take care of your old man. We'll get away, reach some place where they'll never find us.'

'Go with you, Seth Fryer?' she spat at him. 'No!'

His threadbare patience snapped. 'You're worse than your mother, damn you! She was a stubborn bitch, but you . . .' He pulled a grubby piece of rag from his pocket, then he struck a match, watched it flame into life, his sunken eyes glinting with madness. 'You thought I was bluffing, Kathryn Evans, or Kathryn Fryer as it should be. Well, I wasn't.'

He touched the match to the rag, set it burning, then he stepped towards the well.

In the depths, Grant crouched, having heard every word from above. His head was heavy, his limbs sluggish. He shivered in an excess of despair. Suddenly his dazed mind swung to his gun. It had been the gun, tucked into his waistband beneath his shirt, which had been jarred into his ribs when he had fallen; now it offered the only chance he had, but it was no longer in his waistband. Where was it? It must have fallen into the ooze. Faint hope had him searching. For what seemed an age, he thrust his hands about. At last, his fingers closed over the walnut butt and he breathed a sigh of gratitude. Grabbing it up, he thumbed back the hammer, spinning the cylinder to a loaded chamber. He prayed that Fryer would reveal himself, the slightest part of his great bulk, enough to provide a target. But just as he heard the heavy footfall of Fryer from above, the girl's desperate voice came again.

'If I come with you, you'll let him go free?'

Fryer's throaty laugh sounded. 'Thought you'd see sense, my dear.' He paused, his mind debating. 'I'll not let him go free. Can't afford to do that. But I won't fry him to a frizzle. I'll let the bastard take his chances, rot in this hole. Maybe he'll survive, maybe he won't. But it won't be our concern. We'll be miles away before anybody finds him. So you'll come with me, promise to stay with your true daddy, eh?'

Grant didn't hear the girl's response, but he guessed she had nodded her affirmative response. He knew that he would never escape this hole once he was left. He would rot to death and be absorbed into the ooze.

'Just drag these boards over the hole again,' Fryer grunted. 'Can't have Mr Grant getting any fancy ideas.' He stepped towards the opening, paused as the burning rag singed his fingers. He snuffed it out, then stooped to replace the well's covering.

That was when the gun thundered from the depths of the well.

Grant had feared the detonation would spark off flame in the stifling, kerosene-tainted air, but thankfully it did not. Instead, he was left with the reverberation of the detonation bludgeoning his ears. Grant had fired the most important shot of his life and was left with the image of the giant's face disintegrating in a flurry of blood.

The blast of the shot seemed to rumble for an eternity around the confines of the shack, and Kathryn's vision was blurred with red and nauseous green. The latter became paramount, changing to black as she fainted.

She was aroused by the buzz of bluebottles as they took advantage of the corpse, sprawled just six feet from her. She sat up, drawing a trembling hand across her forehead, trying to draw together her addled senses. Then she remembered Grant and she called out his name. There was no response from the depths of the well. She scrambled up, moved around Fryer's lifeless hulk, and clawed back the covering boards, again calling his name.

Grant had lapsed into an exhausted stupor, fearing that somehow Fryer had survived and that all was lost.

Now the girl's cries pierced his consciousness. He raised his head and saw her staring down at him, her eyes pleading for him to respond to her. He saw the tenseness leave her, the expression of relief melt away the alarm from her face . . . and he knew that he had never seen, nor ever would see, a more beautiful and welcome sight.

'Thank God, Grant,' she gasped. 'Oh, thank God!' And then her mind was swinging to more practical matters. 'I'll throw the rope down for you.'

It was not easy hauling himself out of that hole, but

with her help he achieved it, and afterwards they went outside and rested, letting thankfulness for their deliverance sink in. A good hour later, they returned to the fly-thick shack, somehow found the strength to drag Fryer's dead weight to the hole and heave it into the depths, feeling the floor beneath their feet shudder as it struck the ooze. Grant found Fryer's matches and the half-burned rag, then sent Kathryn outside, telling her to stand well back while he completed the final task.

He noticed a heap of branches that Fryer had no doubt gathered in preparation for the murder he'd intended. He dropped them into the depths. He took a deep breath, set flame to the rag and tossed it after the twigs, then he ran for his life.

As he and Kathryn scrambled up the slope, the place erupted from within and soon fire was engulfing the shack's rotting timbers, spiralling dark smoke into the evening sky. They turned their backs and hurried on.

That night they rested beneath a pine, wrapped in a blanket that smelled of horse sweat, yet that did not concern them. Grant was too stunned by all they had experienced to do any more than hold her, while they tried to distance themselves from the past. No useless words broke their communion, no need for anything but silence and understanding, each aware that they had the years ahead.

Come next morning, the whippoorwills awoke them. They looked up to see pearls of dew on the bough above them, and it seemed that each drop reflected a tiny pin-point of hope in the early rays of the sun. He kissed her with a long tenderness.

Presently he recovered the piebald. They refreshed

themselves in a stream and then, riding double, commenced the homeward journey. She took care not to touch his painful ribs, but he enjoyed the feel of her breasts against his back, and the pressure of her head resting on his shoulder.

Half-way to Barclay, they met the mayor and his party. Grant's note had been found, and it was an amazed and relieved Creswell who now heard the complete story. For the first time in days his jovial manner returned.

After marriage to Kathryn, Grant Mayo continued to serve as sheriff of Barclay and he and his wife became respected citizens. It was a noted achievement, during his twenty years as town sheriff, that law was maintained to such a degree, that he was never again obliged to draw a gun in anger.